Praise for Richard Stark and the 1

T0084770

"Richard Stark's Parker . . . is re. always gets away with the swag."

—Stephen King, *Entertainment Weekly*

"Stark was, and is, a pseudonym for Donald Westlake, a writer so inventive and wildly fecund that he had no option but to publish under other names. . . . It's excellent to have [his novels] readily available again—not so much masterpieces of genre, just masterpieces, period."

—Richard Rayner, *L. A. Times*

"If you're looking for crime novels with a lot of punch, try the very, very tough novels featuring Parker by Donald E. Westlake (writing as Richard Stark). *The Hunter*, *The Outfit*, *The Mourner*, and *The Man with the Getaway Face* are all beautifully paced [and] tautly composed."

—James Kaufmann, *The Christian Science Monitor*

"Parker is a brilliant invention. . . . What chiefly distinguishes Westlake, under whatever name, is his passion for process and mechanics. . . . Parker appears to have eliminated everything from his program but machine logic, but this is merely protective coloration. He is a romantic vestige, a free-market anarchist whose independent status is becoming a thing of the past."

—Luc Sante, *The New York Review of Books*

"Richard Stark is the Prince of Noir."

—Martin Cruz-Smith

"One of the most original characters in mystery fiction has returned without a loss of step, savvy, sheer bravado, street smarts, or sense of survival."

—*Mystery News*

"The Parker novels . . . are among the greatest hard-boiled writing of all time."

—*Financial Times* (London)

"Richard Stark (which must be the pseudonym of some long-experienced pro) writes a harsh and frightening story of criminal warfare and vengeance in *The Hunter* with economy, understatement and a deadly amoral objectivity—a remarkable addition to the list of the shockers that the French call *romans noirs*."

—Anthony Boucher, *New York Times Book Review* (1963)

"No one can turn a phrase like Westlake."

—*Detroit News and Free Press*

"Westlake's ability to construct an action story filled with unforeseen twists and quadruple-crosses is unparalleled."

—*San Francisco Chronicle*

The Mourner

The Mourner

RICHARD STARK

With a New Foreword by John Banville

The University of Chicago Press

The University of Chicago Press, Chicago 60637
© 1963 by Richard Stark
Foreword © 2009 by John Banville
All rights reserved.
First published in 1963 by Pocket Books.
Reprinted in 2001 by Mysterious Press.
University of Chicago Press edition 2009

Printed in the United States of America

15 14   5

ISBN-13: 978-0-226-77103-8 (paper)
ISBN-10: 0-226-77103-2 (paper)

Library of Congress Cataloging-in-Publication Data

Stark, Richard, 1933–
    The mourner / Richard Stark ; with a new foreword by John Banville.
        p. cm.
    Summary: The fourth Parker novel has the main character coming up against
the KGB while on the trail of a small statue stolen from a fifteenth-century French
tomb.
    ISBN-13: 978-0-226-77103-8 (pbk. : alk. paper)
    ISBN-10: 0-226-77103-2 (pbk. : alk. paper)   1. Parker (Fictitious character).
I. Banville, John.   II. Title.
    PS3573.E9M6   2009
    813'.54—dc22
                                                          2008042433

♾ The paper used in this publication meets the minimum requirements of the
American National Standard for Information Sciences—Permanence of Paper for
Printed Library Materials, ANSI Z39.48-1992.

THE PARKER NOVELS
John Banville

It was in the 1960s that Richard Stark began writing his masterly series of Parker novels—at last count there were twenty-four of them—but they are as unrepresentative of the Age of Aquarius as it is possible to be. Try imagining this most hardened of hard-boiled criminals in a tie-dyed shirt and velvet bell-bottoms. Parker does not do drugs, having no interest in expanding his mind or deepening his sensibilities; he cares nothing for politics and is indifferent to foreign wars, although he fought or at least took part in one of them; he would rather make money than love and would be willing to give peace a chance provided he could sneak round the back of the love-in and rob everybody's unattended stuff. When he goes to San Francisco it is not to leave his heart there—has Parker got a heart?—but to retrieve some money the Outfit owes him and kill a lot of people in the process.

The appeal of the conventional crime novel is the sense of completion it offers. Life is a mess—we do not remember being born, and death, as Ludwig Wittgenstein wisely observed, is not an experience in life, so that all we have is a chaotic middle, bristling with loose ends, in which nothing is ever properly over and done with. It could be said, of course, that all fiction of whatever genre offers a beginning, middle, and end—even *Finnegans Wake* has a shape—but crime fiction does it best of all. No matter how unlikely the cast of suspects or how baffling the strew of clues in an Agatha Christie whodunit or a Robert Ludlum thriller, we know with a certainty not afforded by real life that when the murderer is unmasked or the conspiracy foiled, everything will click into place, like a jigsaw puzzle assembling itself before our eyes. The Parker books, however, take it as a given that if something can go wrong, it will, and that since something always can go wrong, it invariably does.

Indeed, this is how very many of the Parker stories begin, with things going or gone disastrously awry. And Parker is at his most inventive when at his most desperate.

We first encountered Parker in *The Hunter*, published in 1962. His creator, Donald Westlake, was already an established writer— he adopted the pen name Richard Stark because, as he said in a recent interview, "When you're first in love, you want to do it all the time," and in the early days he was writing so much and so often that he feared the Westlake market would soon become glutted.

Born in 1933, Westlake is indeed a protean writer and, like Parker, the complete professional. Besides crime novels, he has written short stories, comedies, science fiction, and screenplays—his tough, elegant screenplay for *The Grifters*, adapted from a Jim Thompson novel, was nominated for an Academy Award. Surely the finest movie he wrote, however, is *Point Blank*, a noir masterpiece based on the first Parker novel, *The Hunter*, directed by John Boorman and starring Lee Marvin. Anyone who saw the film will consider Marvin the quintessential Parker, though Westlake has said that when he first created his relentless hero—hero?—he imagined him looking more like Jack Palance.

In that first book, *The Hunter*, Parker was a rough diamond—"I'd done nothing to make him easy for the reader," says Westlake, "no small talk, no quirks, no pets"—and looked like a classic pulp fiction hoodlum:

> He was big and shaggy, with flat square shoulders and arms too long in sleeves too short. . . . His hands, swinging curve-fingered at his sides, looked like they were molded of brown clay by a sculptor who thought big and liked veins. His hair was brown and dry and dead, blowing around his head like a poor toupee about to fly loose. His face was a chipped chunk of concrete, with eyes of flawed onyx. His mouth was a quick stroke, bloodless. (p. 3–4)

Even before the end of this short book, however, we see Westlake/Stark begin to cut and burnish his brand-new creation, giving him facets and sharp angles and flashes of a hard, inner fire. He has been betrayed by his best friend and shot by his wife, and now he is owed money by the Outfit—the Mafia, we assume—and he is not going to stop until he has been repaid:

> Momentum kept him rolling. He wasn't sure himself any more how much was a tough front to impress the organization and how much was himself. He knew he was hard, he knew that he worried less about emotion than other people. But he'd never enjoyed the idea of a killing. . . . It was momentum, that was all. Eighteen years in one business, doing

one or two clean fast simple operations a year, living relaxed and easy in
the resort hotels the rest of the time with a woman he liked, and then all
of a sudden it all got twisted around. The woman was gone, the pattern
was gone, the relaxation was gone, the clean swiftness was gone. (p. 171)

The fact is, though Parker himself would be contemptuous of
the notion, he is the perfection of that existential man whose earli-
est models we met in Nietzsche and Kierkegaard and Dostoevsky.
If Parker has ever read Goethe—and perhaps he has?—he will have
recognized his own natural motto in Faust's heaven-defying decla-
ration: "*Im Anfang war die Tat*" [In the beginning was the deed].
Donald Westlake puts it in more homely terms when he says that,
"I've always believed the books are really about a workman at work,
doing the work to the best of his ability," and when in the context
of Parker he refers to "Hemingway's judgment on people, that the
competent guy does it on his own and the incompetents lean on each
other."

In Parker's world there is no law, unless it is the law of the quick
and the merciless against the dim and the slow. The police never ap-
pear, or if they do they are always too late to stop Parker doing what
he is intent on doing. Only twice has he been caught and—briefly
—jailed, once after the betrayal by his wife and Mal Resnick, which
sets *The Hunter* in vengeful motion, and another time in the recent
Breakout. Parker treats the law-abiding world, that tame world where
most of us live, with tight-lipped impatience or, when one or other
of us is unfortunate enough to stumble into his path and hinder him,
with lethal efficiency. Significantly, it is the *idea* of a killing that he
has never enjoyed; this is not to say that he would enjoy the killing
itself, but that he regards the necessity of murder as a waste of essential energies, energies that would be better employed elsewhere.

Violence in the Parker books is always quick and clean and all the more shocking in its swiftness and cleanliness. In one of the books— it would be a spoiler to specify which—Parker forces a young man to dig a hole in the dirt floor of a cellar in search of something buried there, and when the thing has been found, the scene closes with a brief, bald line informing us that Parker shot the young fellow and buried him in the hole he had dug. In another story, Parker and one of his crew tie a hoodlum to a chair and torture some vital information out of him, after which they lock him in a closet, still chair-bound, and depart, indifferent to the fact that no one knows where the hoodlum is and so there will be no one to free him.

With the exception of the likes of James M. Cain, Jim Thompson, and Georges Simenon—that is, the Simenon not of the Maigret books but of what he called his *romans durs*, his hard novels—all crime writers are sentimentalists at heart, even, or especially, when they are at their bloodiest. In conventional tales of murder, mayhem, and the fight for right, what the reader is offered is escape, if only into the dream of a world where men are men and women love them for it, where crooks are crooks and easily identified by the scars on their faces and the Glocks in their fists, where policemen are dull but honest and usually dealing with a bad divorce, where a good man is feared by the lawless and respected by the law-abiding: in short, where life is otherwise and better. In the Parker books, however, it is the sense of awful and immediate reality that makes them so startling, so unsettling, and so convincing.

As the series goes on, Parker has become more intricate in motivation and more polished in manner—his woman, Claire, the replacement for his wife Lynn, the one who shot him and subsequently committed suicide, is a fascinating creation, forbearing, loving, nurturing, the perfect companion for a professional—yet in more than forty years his creator has never allowed him to weaken or to mellow. The most recent caper, *Dirty Money*, published in 2008, ends with a vintage exchange between Parker, a woman, and a grifter who was foolish enough to try pulling a fast one on Parker:

> He helped McWhitney to lie back on the bed, then said to Sandra, "If we do this right, you can get me to Claire's place by two in the morning."
>
> "What a good person I am," she said.
>
> "If you leave me here," the guy on the floor said, "he'll kill me tomorrow morning."
>
> Parker looked at him. "So you've still got tonight," he said.

And that is about as much as Parker, or Richard Stark, is ever willing to allow to anyone.

ONE

1

When the guy with asthma finally came in from the fire escape, Parker rabbit-punched him and took his gun away. The asthmatic hit the carpet, but there'd been another one out there, and he landed on Parker's back like a duffel bag with arms. Parker fell turning, so that the duffel bag would be on the bottom, but it didn't quite work out that way. They landed sideways, joltingly, and the gun skittered away into the darkness.

There was no light in the room at all. The window was a paler rectangle sliced out of blackness. Parker and the duffel bag wrestled around on the floor a few minutes, neither getting an advantage because the duffel bag wouldn't give up his first hold but just clung to Parker's back. Then the asthmatic got his wind and balance back and joined in, trying to kick Parker's head loose. Parker knew the room even in the dark, since he'd lived there

3

the last week, so he rolled over to where he knew there wasn't any furniture. The asthmatic, coming after him, fell over a chair.

Parker rolled to where the wall should be, bumped into it, and climbed up it till he was on his feet, the duffel bag still clinging to his back. The duffel bag's legs were around Parker's hips, and his left arm was around Parker's chest. His right hand kept hitting the side of Parker's head.

Parker moved out to the middle of the room, and then ran backward at the wall. The second time he did it, the duffel bag fell off. Across the room, the asthmatic was still bouncing back and forth amid the furniture. Parker went over that way, got the asthmatic silhouetted against the pale rectangle of the window, and clipped him. The asthmatic went down, hitting furniture on the way.

Parker waited a few seconds, holding his breath, but he couldn't hear anybody moving, so he went over and shut and locked the window, pulled the venetian blinds, and switched on the table lamp beside the bed.

The room was a mess. One bed had been turned at a forty-five-degree angle to the wall, and the mattress was half-pulled off the other one. The dresser was shoved out of position so it was blocking the closet door, and the wastebasket lay on its side in the middle of the floor with a big dent in it. All four chairs were knocked over. One of them had both wooden arms broken.

Parker walked through the mess to see what he'd landed.

Fifteen minutes ago it had started, with Parker lying clothed on the bed in the darkness, thinking about one thing and another, and waiting for Handy to come back. That was after eleven o'clock, so Handy was late already. The lights were off because Parker liked it that way, and the window was open because November nights in Washington, D.C., are cool but pleasant. Then through the window had come the faint clatter of somebody mounting the fire escape, four flights below at street level. Parker had got off the bed and listened at the window. The somebody came up the fire escape about as quiet as the Second World War but trying to be quieter, and stopped at Parker's floor. Somebody with asthma. It was all so amateurish, Parker couldn't take it seriously, which is why the second one surprised him. He'd waited, and the guy with asthma had waited outside—probably to make sure there wasn't anybody home in Parker's room—and then finally he came in and it all had started.

The nice thing about a hotel. Nobody questions any noise that lasts less than ten minutes.

They were both out, the duffel bag on his face and the asthmatic on his back. Parker looked them over one at a time, and then frisked them.

The asthmatic was short, scrubby, wrinkled as a prune, and fifty or more, with the withered look of a wino. He was wearing baggy gray pants, a flannel shirt that had once been plaid but had now faded down to a gray like the pants, and a dark-blue double-breasted suit coat with all but one button missing and the shoulder padding sagging down into the arms. He had white wool socks on and brown oxfords with holes in the soles.

Parker went through his pockets. In the right-hand coat pocket he found a boy-scout knife with all the attachments—a screwdriver, nail file, corkscrew, everything but a useful blade—and in the left-hand pocket a hotel key. The board attached to the key was marked: HOTEL REGAL 27. In the shirt pocket was a crumpled pack of Camels and in the left-hand pants pocket forty-seven cents in change. From the hip pocket he took a bedraggled old child's wallet of imitation alligator skin, with a two-color picture of a cowboy on a bucking bronco on one side and a horseshoe on the other. Inside the wallet was a hundred dollars in new tens and four dollars in old singles, plus half a dozen movie-theater ticket stubs, a long, narrow photo of a burlesque dancer named Fury Feline, clipped from a newspaper, and a Social Security card and membership card in Local 802, International Alliance of Chefs and Kitchen Helpers. The Social Security card and the union card were made to James F. Wilcoxen.

That was all. Parker left Wilcoxen and went over to the duffel bag, who had started to move. He had long, straight, limp hair, dry blond in color, and Parker grabbed a handful of it and slapped his head against the floor. He stopped moving. Parker rolled him over.

This one was just as short, and maybe even thinner, but about twenty years younger, with the face of a ferret. He was dressed all in black. Black shoes and socks, black pegged trousers, black wool-knit sweater. He had long, thin fingers and narrow feet.

Parker searched him. Under the black sweater was a blue cotton shirt, and in the pocket was a pair of sunglasses. The right-hand pants pocket contained fifty-six cents in change and a key to room 29 in Hotel Regal; the left, a roll of bills—one hundred dollars in new tens. Left hip pocket, a Beretta Jaguar .22, with the three-and-a-half-inch barrel. Right hip pocket, a wallet containing seven dollars, plus a bunch of dog-eared clippings about the various arrests of Donald Scorbi on suspicion of this and that, mostly assault or drunk and disorderly, with one narcotics possession. The wallet also disgorged a laminated reduced photostat of a Navy discharge—general discharge, for medical reasons—with the same name on it, Donald Scorbi.

Parker kept the two stacks of new tens and the Beretta, but put everything else back in Scorbi's and Wilcoxen's pockets. Then he used their shoelaces to tie their hands behind them, and their belts to secure their ankles together. Scorbi started to come out of it again and he had to be put back to sleep, but Wilcoxen was still out, wheezing through his open mouth.

Parker looked them over, and decided to keep Wilcoxen. He used a washcloth and face towel to gag Scorbi, then dragged him into the bathroom and dumped him in the tub. He closed the door and searched around the room for the other gun, the one he'd taken from Wilcoxen early in the scuffle.

It was under the dresser, a Smith & Wesson Terrier, five-shot .32. Parker took it and the Beretta and stowed them away in his suitcase. His watch said eleven-thirty-five, which made Handy over half an hour late, so something had gone wrong.

Parker straightened the room and Wilcoxen still hadn't come out of it. Parker dragged him over to the wall, propped him up in a sitting position, and pinched him awake. Wilcoxen came out of it complaining, groaning and thrashing his head around and keeping his eyes tight shut. There was a sour smell of wine on his breath. His face was all wrinkled gray leather except for two bright red circles on his cheeks, like a clown's makeup.

Parker said, "Open your eyes, Jimmy."

Wilcoxen stopped complaining and opened his eyes. They were a wet, washed-out blue, like an overexposed color photo. He took a while getting them to focus on Parker's face, and then the red blotches on his cheeks got suddenly redder, or the rest of the face paler.

Parker said, "Good," then straightened up and went away across the room to the nearest chair. He brought it over and sat down and kicked Wilcoxen conversationally in the ribs. "We'll talk."

Wilcoxen's lips were wet. He shook his head and blinked a lot.

Parker said, "I got a partner. You had a partner. Scorbi."

Wilcoxen looked around and didn't see Scorbi.

"Your partner wouldn't tell me about my partner. I threw him back out the window."

Wilcoxen's eyes got bigger. He stared at Parker and waited, but Parker didn't have anything else to say. The silence got thicker, and Wilcoxen squirmed a lot. His feet jiggled, and he licked his lips and kept blinking. Parker sat looking at him, waiting, but Wilcoxen's eyes kept darting all over the place.

Finally, he asked, "What you want from me?"

Parker shook his head and kicked him again. "Wrong answer."

"I don't know no partner. Honest to Christ."

"What *do* you know?"

"I got a hundred bucks. Donny and me both. Go to the Wynant Hotel, first fire escape in the alley, fifth floor. If there's nobody home, take everything there. Suitcases and like that."

"And if there's somebody home?"

"Don't do nothing. Come back and report."

"Back where?"

Wilcoxen's blinking was getting worse. His eyes were closed more than they were open. "Listen," he said. "It's just a job, you know? A hundred bucks. Nobody hurt, just pick up some suitcases. Anybody woulda took it."

Parker shook his head. He didn't care about that. "Back where?" he asked.

"Howison Tavern. On E Street, down by Fourth Precinct."

"Who do you see?"

Wilcoxen frowned, and the blinking settled down a little. "I don't know," he said. "He just told us go in there and sit down. If we got the stuff, somebody would come by, pick it up. If not, somebody would come by, get the report."

"What time you supposed to be there?"

"By one o'clock."

"Which E Street?"

"Huh? Oh, Southeast."

"Who gave you the job?"

"The job? Listen, I got pins and needles in my hands."

Parker looked at his watch. Quarter to twelve. He had an hour and fifteen minutes. "I'm in a hurry, Jimmy," he said.

"How come you know my name?"

Parker kicked him in the ribs again, not hard, just as a reminder.

"I'm giving you the straight story. I ain't going to lie for a hundred bucks. You didn't have to throw Donny out no window."

"Who gave you the job?"

"Oh, uh—a guy named Angel. He's a heavy, he hangs out around North Capitol Street, up behind the station. Donny and me, we was in a movie on D Street, and when we come out Angel grabs onto us and gives us the offer."

"Is Angel going to be at the Howison Tavern?"

"He says no. He says somebody will come by, don't worry, he'll recognize us. We should sit in a booth and drink beer. Schlitz."

"Where do I find this Angel?"

"I don't know. Honest to Christ. Hangin' around someplace, up around behind the station. In around there, you know."

It was no good. Parker thought it over, chewing his lip. The meeting couldn't be faked, so there was no way to start a trail from there. And it would take more than an hour and a quarter to find somebody named Angel hanging around the Union Station area somewhere. If Handy was still alive, he'd be alive till one o'clock. Then, when Scorbi and Wilcoxen didn't show up, whoever had Handy would know there was trouble. The easiest thing would be dump Handy.

So it had to be done from the other direction, through the girl.

Parker nodded to himself. "All right, Jimmy," he said. "You can go. Roll over so I can untie you."

"You mean it? Honest to Christ?"

"Hurry, Jimmy."

Wilcoxen scramble away from the wall and flopped over on his stomach.

"You're all right, honest to Christ you are. You know it wasn't nothing personal. There wasn't even supposed to be nobody here, just suitcases and like that. We ain't torpedoes or nothing."

"I know," Parker said. He untied Wilcoxen's hands and stepped back. "Undo your ankles yourself."

Wilcoxen had trouble making his hands work. While he was loosening the belt from around his ankles and putting his shoelaces back in his shoes, Parker got the Terrier out of the suitcase, and held it casually where Wilcoxen could see it. He left the Beretta where it was; he didn't like .22's much.

When Wilcoxen got to his feet, Parker said, "Scorbi's in the bathroom. Go untie him."

Wilcoxen suddenly smiled, beaming from ear to ear. "I knew you didn't throw Donny out no window," he said. He hurried over and opened the bathroom door. "Donny! He's lettin' us go, Donny!"

After a while Scorbi came out, walking lame like

Wilcoxen. He looked sullen, not joining in Wilcoxen's happiness. Parker said, "Out the way you came in."

"What about our dough?" Scorbi asked.

"Hurry," Parker said.

"Come on, Donny," said Wilcoxen. He tugged at Scorbi's sleeve. "Come on, let's go."

"Our rods and our dough."

Parker said, "Go on, Jimmy. Either he follows you or he don't."

Wilcoxen hurried over and climbed out the window onto the fire escape. Scorbi hung back a second, but then he shrugged and went out the window. The two of them started down the fire escape, making even more noise than they had coming up.

Parker stowed the Terrier away inside his coat and picked up the phone. When the operator came on, he made his voice high-pitched and nervous. "There's somebody on the fire escape! Get the police! Hurry! They're going down the fire escape!"

He hung up while the operator was still asking questions, switched off the light, and left the room. He took the elevator down and crossed the lobby and went outside. A prowl car was parked down to the left, with the red light flashing. Hotels get fast service.

Parker stood on the sidewalk, and a couple of minutes later two cops came out of the alley alongside the hotel, pushing Scorbi and Wilcoxen in front of them. So that was that. Because the Scorbis and Wilcoxens never talk to the law, it couldn't get back to Parker. So, no matter how good a story they thought up, they'd miss that one-o'clock meeting, and whoever had Handy wouldn't be warned. It was better even than keeping them tied up in the bathroom.

Parker turned and walked the other way. A block later he hailed a cab.

2

It was just over the Maryland line, in Silver Spring, a squat, faded apartment building called Sligo Towers. Built of dark brick aged even darker, the bricks widely separated by the plaster, it looked like an old Thirties standing set left over on the Universal back lot. Thirties-like imitations of Gay Nineties gaslights, containing twenty-five-watt bulbs, flanked the arched entrance to the courtyard.

The courtyard was just concrete, but pink coloring had been added before it set. It was bounded on three sides by the building, rising eight stories and sprouting air conditioners here and there like acne. On the fourth side was a double arch with a concrete pillar, separating courtyard from sidewalk. Beyond, dark cars slept at the curb, hoods mutely reflecting the street light from down the block. A car purred by, without pausing.

Parker turned the far corner and came striding toward the Sligo Towers. He wore a gray suit and a figured shirt, the suit coat open despite the night chill. He looked like a businessman, in a tough business. He could have been a liquor salesman in a dry state, or the automobile-company vice-president who takes away the dealerships, or maybe the business manager of one of the unions with the big buildings downtown around the Capitol. He could have been a hard, lean businessman coming home from a late night at the office.

He turned at the double arch and went into the court-yard, his shoes with the rubber soles and heels making no sound on the pink concrete. There were walls on three sides of him, all around the courtyard, with a door in each wall. Each was marked with a letter so rococo it looked like a drawing of an ivy-covered window.

He didn't know which door. Slowing down would spoil the effect, stopping would tip any watcher that he was a stranger here. He kept on toward "B," the door straight ahead. Three brick-lined pink concrete steps led up, and then the door was metal, painted to look like wood. It was a double door, and inside there was a metal bar like those found on the doors of schools and theaters. A half flight of metal stairs painted red led up to a hall-way running at right angles. There was no interior door, which was a surprise. With no trouble at all, he was al-ready in the building.

Facing the stairs, on the wall, was a double row of brass mailboxes, with name plates. Parker read the names, but didn't find the one he wanted. He looked to right and left, and in both directions the hallway ended short at apartment doors, so the three sections of the building weren't connected at this level. They would be, in the basement. He went back down the half flight to a longer hallway, this one walled with rough plaster and dimly lit. He turned left.

At the end, the hallway made a right angle to the left. Parker followed it, came to another flight of stairs, and went up. He was now in section A, and the name he wanted was under the fifth mailbox from the left on the bottom row. Miss Clara Stoper. Apartment 26.

There were four apartments to a floor, so 26 would be on the seventh floor. The elevator was to the right of the mailboxes. Parker got out at the seventh floor. Apartment 26 was to the left. Parker moved down that way and listened at the door, but could hear nothing. There was a thin crack between the bottom of the door and the floor, but no light showed through.

Parker rang the bell. There was no peephole in the door, so he waited where he was, in front of the door. Nothing happened for a while, so he rang the bell again. Then he saw light under the door, and a bolt clicked.

He frowned, trying to remember the name Handy was using with her. Pete Castle, that was it.

The door opened a few inches, held by a chain from opening any farther. A chain like that can't keep anyone out; it only serves as an irritation. Beyond was a sleepy-eyed girl's face. She was sleepy-eyed and holding a robe closed at her throat, but her hairdo was in perfect shape without a net.

"Who is it? What do you want?" she said, the voice a good imitation of sleepy blurriness.

But the hairdo had given it away. Parker didn't have to ask questions after all. His right foot went out and wedged in the doorway, so the door couldn't be closed. His right hand reached through and grabbed a handful of hair on the top of her head. He slammed her forehead against the edge of the door. Her hands started to come up toward his wrist, and her mouth was opening wide to shout, so he did it again. The third time, she became a dead weight and collapsed straight downward, leaving several strands of hair in his fist.

It took two high, flat kicks with his heel to pop the chain loose from the doorpost. The door swung open, and beyond the lighted foyer and the dark living room was a bright doorway. The silhouette of a fat man appeared in it and Parker dove for the rug, stabbing into his pocket for the Terrier. The fat man fired over his head. Parker rolled into a wall and came up with the Terrier in his hand. The bright doorway was empty. Parker moved quickly, slamming the hall door and flicking off the foyer light.

The fat man had the same idea. There wasn't any bright doorway any more. The whole apartment was dark.

The fat man knew this place, and Parker didn't. The fat man could sit and wait, and Parker couldn't take the time. The fat man could stay where he was and listen, shoot at the first sound, or just wait for Parker to go away.

In the dark, Parker found the unconscious girl. He dragged her into the living room and knelt beside her on one knee. In a conversational voice he said, "Fat man. Listen to me, fat man. You fired one shot. The light sleepers around here are awake now; they think it was a truck making a backfire. You turn on a light, fat man, and you come out here where I can see you, or I make more noises. I can scream like a woman, and then very slow I can empty this pistol into your girl. Too many backfires, fat man. Somebody will call the police. Before I'm finished, somebody will call the police. Then I wipe the gun clean and put it down on the floor and beat it. No fingerprints of mine here, fat man. Nothing to connect me. But your fingerprints are everywhere. And somebody'll connect you up with this woman."

Silence.

"Now, fat man. The next thing I do is scream like a woman."

"Wait."

It was a soft voice, and from the left somewhere. Not in the room.

"Hurry."

"I will not turn on the lights," said the voice. It had a faint accent, something Middle European. "But it is possible we can talk."

"Not in the dark."

"You must be reasonable. We will effect a compromise."

"Name it."

"You want something here, quite obviously, else you wouldn't have come. Yet I don't know you. I cannot imagine what it is you want. Your reactions and movements are hardly those of a burglar or a rapist. Either you have come to murder me, at the behest of the opposition, or you are here seeking information of some sort. If murder is your purpose, it would hardly be sensible for me to show myself. If what you want is information, we can discuss it just as profitably in the dark."

While the fat man was talking, Parker was crawling toward the sound of his voice, moving cautiously across the carpet on hands and knees. When the voice stopped, Parker stopped. He turned his head away, so he wouldn't sound any closer. "I'm here for information. Where's Pete Castle?"

"Ah!" The fat man seemed pleased to have the mystery cleared up. "He *did* have associates."

"Where is he?"

"Reposing in a safe place, I assure you. And relatively unharmed. I would suggest, by the way, that you come no closer. You are now nearly to the doorway, and I pride myself on my shooting. If you clear that doorway, and then are foolish enough to speak, it will take me no more than one backfire to dispose of you."

"Why warn me?"

"Curiosity, just curiosity. The same motive that impelled me to have your friend taken away to where he could be questioned at leisure. Our operation is of a complexity and a delicacy. Your friend's presence became, quite naturally, of concern to us. We had to know whether his goal coincided with our own. Now I discover that there are two of you, perhaps more. You might tell me just what it is you want with Kapor. If our purposes are the same, it is possible we could come to an agreement."

"All I want is Pete Castle. You'll tell me where to find him, or I'll start making that noise—"

A body suddenly fell on him, grappling with him, and the girl's voice shrilled in his ear, "I've got him, Mr. Menlo! I've got him, I've got him!"

Parker struggled with her, hampered by the darkness, and over her shouting he heard the pounding of running feet. He flung her off at the last in time to catch a glimpse of the hall door opening, and the back of the fat man. Parker headed that way, but the girl got him around the ankles, dropping him again. He kicked free, made it to the hallway, and heard the clatter of taps on metal stairs. The fat man was already halfway down.

Parker ran back into the apartment, switching on lights as he went. The girl was slowly and groggily getting to her feet. Her robe was disarranged, and beneath it she was fully dressed except for shoes. Parker ran past her to the first window he found, in the kitchen, but it faced the rear of the building. So did the bedroom window. No window faced the courtyard.

Parker came back to the living room. The girl was on her feet but weaving, moving at a snail's pace toward the door. Parker came after her, grabbed her by a shoulder, flung her back into the living room. The chain attachment on the front door was broken but the bolt still worked. Parker shot it, and went back to the living room.

The girl was no more than half-conscious. She'd been battered once too often in the last five minutes. She was standing in the middle of the room, frowning and squinting as though not sure what was going on. Parker took hold of her arm and steered her into the kitchen.

She moved with no complaint, repeating under her breath, "Mr. Menlo? Mr. Menlo?"

Parker sat her on a kitchen chair and slapped her face to get her attention. "Where have they got Pete Castle?"

She frowned up at him, and then rationality came back to her and her face hardened. "You can just go to hell."

Parker shook his head in irritation. He hated this kind of thing, hurting people to make them talk. It was messy and time-consuming and there ought to be a better way. But there wasn't.

He found twine in a kitchen drawer, and tied her to the chair, and gagged her. She fought it, but not successfully. He left her right hand free and put paper and pencil on the table.

"Write the address when you're ready," he said. Then he reached for the kitchen matches.

3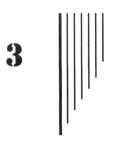

There was a delivery truck out front, a small, dark panel truck with the name KELSON FURNITURE on the sides. It was way after one o'clock, but two men in white coveralls were carrying a rolled-up rug out of the dark bungalow.

This was in Cheverly, off Landover Road. Parker crouched in the back seat of the cab, watching them through the windshield. They were half a block ahead, and on the other side of the street. Just the two men in white coveralls and the rolled-up rug. No fat man.

Parker said, "Douse your lights."

It was a lady cab driver, a small, middle-aged black woman with a wild red hat. She glared over her shoulder at him. "What was that?"

Parker found a twenty and shoved it at her, wishing he had the Pontiac. But Handy had taken that with him. Parker said, "I want you to put out your lights. Then follow that delivery truck over there when it takes off."

She now looked baffled, but just as suspicious. "Is this some kind of gag, mister?"

"No gag."

"We're not supposed to do nothing like that."

"Just take the twenty."

"How I know you ain't a cop? Or a inspector or something?"

"Do I look like a cop?"

"Some cops, yeah."

"All right," Parker said. "We'll do it the hard way." He dropped the twenty in her lap and showed her the Terrier.

The gun she could understand. She doused the lights. "If you got robbery or rapery on your mind, big man," she said, "you just forget it."

"All you do is follow that delivery truck. Get ready now."

"Sure. They got a body in that rug." She thought she was being scornful.

"That's right," Parker answered.

"Huh?"

The delivery truck started away from the curb. Parker said, "Give them a block. Keep the lights off till I say so. You can see by the street lights."

"If I get stopped by a cop—"

"Don't worry about it."

The cab, with its headlights off, trailed the taillights of the delivery truck out to Landover Road, where the truck turned back toward the city. As soon as it had made the turn and was out of sight, Parker said, "Put your lights on now."

The truck barreled along ahead of them, and didn't seem aware it was being followed. There was no circling of blocks, or speeding up and slowing down, to check for a possible tail. The truck just ran on over to Bladensburg road and down into the city. In the Trinidad section it made a right turn. Parker said, "Keep back a block and a half unless they turn."

Ahead, the truck turned in at a driveway. This was a commercial section, shut down tight. Parker said, "Turn at the corner here. Don't go past where they turned in. Now go half a block and stop."

He had another twenty ready when the cab stopped. He tossed it to her. "This one's to forget to call the cops."

She shrugged and shook her head. "I sure hope you got your money's worth," she said. She sounded doubtful.

Parker hurried back around the corner, and down the block toward where the truck had turned in. There was no reason to hurry, except he wanted to know what the hell was going on.

One thing he knew now—Handy was still alive. If

Handy were dead, they'd either have left him there or driven the body further away from town. But he was alive, because they still wanted to know what he was up to, and they'd just moved him so they could question him some more. The fat man had hurried away, then set up this new place to bring Handy and called his friends to get Handy out of there. If Parker had taken three minutes longer getting the answers out of the girl, he'd have missed the move completely.

Whether Handy was alive or dead wasn't the important part. The important part was who these people were and what they wanted. If they were after the mourner too, it would complicate things.

Parker came to the driveway. It was blacktop and narrow, hemmed in on both sides by brick walls. The one on the right was a garage and on the left was a dry cleaner's. From the front, both looked dark and empty.

Parker moved cautiously down the driveway and found the truck at the end, against another wall. The truck doors were open, and the rug was gone.

Both side walls contained metal doors back here. Parker tried the one leading to the garage first, and it was unlocked. He stepped through into darkness, and listened. A dim murmur of voices came from his right and above. He moved that way, skirting first a workbench and then some machinery, and ahead of him saw a dim light. The ceiling was high, and a row of offices was built out from the rear wall, with a wooden staircase going up. The light was spilling down from one of the offices.

Parker moved forward, and then saw a cigarette glow for a second ahead of him. There was somebody sitting at the foot of the stairs.

Parker moved in slowly, staying back under the stairs, which had been built hastily, without risers. Parker held the Terrier by the barrel, reached through between two of the stairs, and put the guard out with the gun butt. He slumped, and slid off the stairs to the floor.

Parker came around and checked him, and he was out. The voices were still murmuring upstairs, without a break. He went up the stairs, the butt of the Terrier in his hand now, and followed the sound of the voices.

There was a walkway outside the offices, with the office wall on one side and a wooden railing on the other. The wall was paneling halfway up, and glass the rest of the way. The light was coming through the glass down toward the other end of the walkway. Parker moved that way, and edged close enough to look in through the glass.

It was just a small office, with pale-green filing cabinets and pale-green partitions. There was a desk, and three chairs, and the usual office furniture, with a big calendar on the back wall showing a trout leaping in a mountain stream.

They had Handy sitting on the floor, his back against the wall under the calendar. He was tied with a lot of white clothesline, but not gagged. There was blood on his face, and his clothes were messed up. The two men in the white coveralls were with him, talking to him. Handy's eyes were shut, but from his posture he was probably awake. Or mostly awake.

Parker couldn't quite hear what they were saying. And he was surprised that the fat man wasn't there with them. But the way the fat man could run, he maybe never got too close to the action. He just stayed back by a telephone somewhere where he could be the general.

Parker turned back and retraced his steps. There was only one door leading into the offices, but each had connecting doors. Parker stepped into one from the walkway and moved along through three other dark offices, opening and closing doors as he went without a sound. Then he was at the partition, standing in front of the inner door to the lighted office, and he could hear now.

". . . but now we've got plenty of time. We've got all night, you know that? That partner of yours is plenty good, catching on so quick, but how's he gonna find you here? Even if he gets anything out of Clara, so what? Off he goes to the house in Cheverly, right? And there's the dead end."

The other one said, "Or maybe you got another partner. How many of you in this thing, Pete? Just the two of you? Or maybe three, four? What do you say, Pete?"

There was silence, and then a thud, and the first voice said, "Take it easy, boy. You want to put him out again?"

"All he has to do is be civil, that's all. Just answer a polite question, that's all."

"I tell you what, we'll go over it for him again. Maybe he's just a slow study."

"Let me take my pliers to his fingers. He'll be a real quick study."

"No, Mr. Menlo said don't mess him up too bad till we find out what the score is."

"You *got* to mess him up. Look at him."

"I figure he'll listen to reason. Isn't that right, Pete? You know we can't do nothing drastic to you, but Pete boy, we got all night. Like, I could just take your hair like this, and just real gentle rap your head on the wall, see? Boom. And then again. Boom. See? The first time ain't so bad. The second time's a little worse. Now the third time. Boom. See? What do you think, Pete? Maybe forty times? We got all night, Pete."

"So boom him and get it over."

"Now wait a minute, let me talk to him. We got interrupted before; let me talk to him. Pete, listen to me. We don't want so much. We ain't greedy, Pete. But just listen. We're getting this operation set up, getting everything ready, and all of a sudden you come into the middle of it. You make a play for Clara, so pretty soon Clara's got it figured what you're after is to get into Kapor's house. You're working on something and we're working on something. Now, all we want to know, Pete—is it the same something? What do you want in Kapor's house, Pete? And how many of you are in it? That's all we want to know. What the hell, Pete, we were here first. I mean, fair's fair, right? Boom, Pete. Boom. Isn't fair fair, Pete? Boom, Pete."

There was no sense listening to any more. They wouldn't be saying more about themselves. There was Clara, and fat man, Menlo, and these two, plus the one downstairs and maybe the one named Angel. Maybe some others too. They were all after something that Kapor had, just as Parker was, and if they, like Parker, were after the mourner, they wouldn't be volunteering that information to Handy. So Parker opened the door and went into the light, gun first. "Freeze."

Nobody ever does. The two of them spun around, shock-eyed, and Handy opened tired eyes and grinned.

"Untie him," Parker said.

The conversational one did it, while the one with impatient pliers stood there and glowered. Then Parker had the one with the impatient pliers use the same ropes to tie up the conversational one. Parker only wanted to take one with him, and he had decided to take Pliers because in his experience the people who were the most anxious to use torture were also the ones most anxious to talk instead of being tortured themselves. Parker had been forced to ask questions the hard way twice already tonight. It hadn't been bad with Wilcoxen, but with the woman, Clara, it had been very bad, because she was stubborn and Parker was in a hurry.

Handy couldn't walk; his legs were numb from being tied so tight for so long. Parker had Pliers carry Handy, and the three of them left the office and went downstairs and out to the truck. Parker got the ignition key, and then arranged the three of them. There was no partition between the seats and the load area, so Handy lay in back with the Browning .380 automatic Parker had taken away from the conversational one upstairs. From there he could keep an eye on Pliers, in front. Parker drove.

He backed the truck down the driveway to the street, but for a second he didn't know where to go. They hadn't set up any place private yet, because the job wasn't that close to being ready, and the hotel room wouldn't be any good for questioning Pliers. Then Parker remembered the bungalow where they'd been holding Handy. Why not? If any place in the District was guaranteed empty right now, it was that bungalow.

They drove in silence. Parker had his questions, but he wanted the proper atmosphere in which to ask them.

And among them, he was wondering if Harrow had been dumb enough to send two teams after the same ball. Could the fat man and his friends be working for Harrow too? That would be stupid, and dangerous, for everybody.

But Harrow wasn't all that smart. . . .

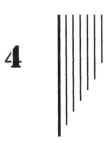

4

That was two months ago.

For eighteen years, Parker had lived the way he wanted, to a pattern he liked. He was a heavy gun, in on one or two institutional robberies a year—a bank, or a payroll, or an armored car—just often enough to keep the finances fat, and the rest of the time he lived in resort hotels on either coast, with a cover that would satisfy even the income-tax beagles. Then, because of a snafu in one job, he'd got fouled up with the syndicate.* He'd thought he'd got that straightened out—he'd even picked up a new face from a plastic surgeon†—and then, two months before in Miami, a syndicate heavy had tried for him, in his own hotel room, late at night. There'd

*The Hunter
†The Man With the Getaway Face

been a girl in the bed with him named Bett Harrow, and when the syndicate heavy died, Bett had taken off with the gun that had helped kill him. The gun could be traced to Parker's cover name, Charles Willis, and that was bad. There was a lot of money and time and preparation tied up in that cover.

Bett had let him know he could have the gun back for a price, but he'd told her she had to wait while he got the syndicate off his back. He'd got in touch with Handy McKay, who'd worked with him on other jobs in the past, and this time the syndicate question was settled for good.‡ Then Parker went back to Miami with Handy to find out what Bett Harrow wanted.

But it wasn't Bett who wanted anything, it was her father. Parker set up the meeting, but left Handy out of it. It might be useful sometime if neither Bett nor her father knew anything about Handy.

The Harrows came to Parker's hotel room at one-thirty in the afternoon. They knocked on the door and when Parker opened it there was Bett, tall and slender and blonde, with vicious good looks, and next to her an older man, short and stocky and gray-haired. He had no tan at all, and the suit he was wearing was too heavy for Miami Beach, so he'd obviously just arrived in town. He was looking uncomfortable and carrying a book under his arm.

‡The Outfit

Bett said, "Can we come in, Chuck?"

He motioned them in. Bett came in first, and her father followed, clutching the book protectively to his chest. It was a large, slender book with a red binding and a picture on the cover of some people in a balloon.

"Dad, this isn't Chuck Willis, but he says he is." Bett was enjoying herself. It was the kind of scene she liked, which was one of the reasons she was living on alimony.

Ralph Harrow was fifty-three, the principal stockholder of the Commauck Aircraft Company. He owned 27 percent of that company's outstanding shares. And he was additionally a large stockholder in three airlines and one insurance company. He was also a member of the board of each of the five companies thus represented in his stock portfolio. He had been born to money, and had multiplied his inheritance. A staff of attorneys saw to it that nothing he did was technically illegal, and they earned their money.

He came into the room showing an unusual apprehension, and responded to his daughter's introductions with a brief, wary nod. "This is my daughter's idea, uh, Willis," he said. "I assure you, coercion is not my normal, uh, my normal policy."

"You haven't coerced me yet," Parker had answered. "First you got to tell me what you want."

Harrow licked his lips and glanced at his daughter,

but she was no help. "To begin with, I'd like you to read a brief article in this magazine."

He said magazine, but it was obviously the book he meant. He held it up, and Parker saw above the picture a title: *Horizon*. And below the picture a date: September, 1958. So it was a magazine that looked like a book.

Harrow opened the magazine-book, muttering to himself, "Page sixty-two." He found the page and extended the open book.

Parker shrugged, not taking the book. "Just tell me what you want."

If it had been just the father he'd been dealing with, he'd squeeze the gun out of him now and throw him away. But the daughter was tougher stuff.

Harrow was looking pained, as though he had indigestion. "It would really be quicker if you'd read this first," he said.

"Go on, Chuck," Bett said. "It's short."

"Just two pages," Harrow added.

Parker said, "You read it, didn't you?"

"Well . . . yes."

"So you can tell me about it."

Parker turned away from the book and went over to sit at the writing desk, turning the chair around to face the room.

Bett was still smiling. She settled luxuriantly on the

bed, catlike, and said, "You might as well do it his way, Dad. I don't think Chuck's a reader."

"Well, but . . ." Harrow was confused and unhappy; this wasn't the way he'd planned things.

Parker had had enough waiting around. "Either get to the point or get out," he said.

Bett said softly, "And go to the police?"

"If you want. I don't give a damn."

Bett laughed, and looked challengingly at her father. Harrow sighed. "Very well. It would have been easier if you'd . . . but very well. This article concerns a group of eighty-two statuettes in a monument at Dijon, in France." He turned the book around so Parker could see. "You see the title? 'The Missing Mourners of Dijon,' by Fernand Auberjonois."

"You want me to steal a statue," Parker said, and Bett laughed again.

"I want you to understand the background." Harrow answered unhappily. "It is important that you under-stand the background."

"Why?"

"Dear Dad's a romantic," said Bett, with honeyed venom in her smile.

Parker shrugged. He didn't care what the Harrow family thought of each other.

"These statuettes, eighty-two of them, were made for the tomb of John the Fearless and Philip the Good,

Dukes of Burgundy," Harrow said. "John was murdered in 1419, but not before ordering the tomb to be built. Philip was his son, and survived till 1467, when he—"

"The statues," Parker said.

"Yes. The statues. They are sixteen inches high, made of alabaster, and were placed in niches at the base of the two memorials. No two of them are precisely alike, and they all express an attitude of mourning. Every possible variation on mourning, both true and false. There are monks, priests, choirboys—Well. At any rate, they are priceless. And at the time of the French Revolution, many of them were stolen or lost. At the present time, seventy-four of the statuettes are still in Dijon; some were always there, others have been found and returned. Of the remaining eight, one is owned by a private collector in France, two by a private collector in this country, in Ohio, and two are in the Cleveland Museum. The other three mourners are still missing."

He closed the book, but kept his finger in the place. "That's what this article would have told you," he said, "and just as quickly as I have told it to you."

Parker waited, controlling his impatience. None of this was necessary. Harrow wanted a statue stolen, that was the point. If the job looked easy enough, and if the price was right, he might do it. Otherwise, no. All this talk was a waste of time.

But Harrow wasn't finished yet. "Now, for you to understand what I want, and why I want it, you must understand something about me."

"Why?"

Bett said, "Let him, Chuck. It's the only way he knows how to talk."

"Elizabeth, please."

"Get on with it," Parker said.

"Very well. Very well. I, Mr. Willis, am in a very small and special way a collector of medieval statuary. I say in a special way. My collection is small, but if I do say so myself it's excellent. I have at present only eight pieces. This is because my criteria are very high indeed. Each piece must be unique, must be one of a kind, must have no counterpart anywhere in the world. Each must be valued so highly as to be for all practical purposes priceless. And each must have an unusual and fascinating history. My daughter is right, Mr. Willis—I am a romantic. I am fascinated by each piece in my collection, by its creation and by its history. You understand this collection is for my own satisfaction, and not on display."

Bett laughed and said, "Because they were all stolen."

"Not so!" Harrow looked indignantly at his daughter. "Every piece was paid for, and handsomely too."

"But the *fascinating history*," she said, mocking the words. "It always includes a theft or two, doesn't it?"

"That is not at *all* my concern. I myself have—"

"Shut up," said Parker.

They stopped their bickering at once, and looked at him startled. "You want me to steal one of these statues, right? From a museum?"

"Good heavens, no!" Harrow seemed honestly shocked. "In the first place, Willis, all the statuettes mentioned in this article are far too easily traceable. They're *unique*, you see, each a separate and distinct figure. Here, look." He came forward, opening the book again, shoving it under Parker's nose. "Here are pictures of some of them. See? They're all different."

Five of the statuettes were pictured, and Parker looked at them, nodding. Five sad, robed, weeping mournful little people, in five different postures of grief.

"Besides," added Harrow, "besides, none of these has the kind of history I mean, the sort of background I want for the pieces in my collection."

Parker shoved the book away. "What then?"

"Let me tell you." Harrow stood in front of him, suddenly beaming, a glint of excitement in his eyes. "You remember, three of the mourners are still missing? No one knows where they are. But I've located one of them!"

"And that's the one you want me to get?"

"Yes. Yes. Now, the way it—"

"Sit down. You're making me nervous."

"Oh, of course. I'm sorry. Yes, of course."

Harrow retreated, and sat poised on the edge of the chair by the door. Parker's tone had drained some of the excitement out of him, and he went on more normally. "The way I happened to discover this mourner was rather odd. My company, about three years ago, received a small order for cargo planes from Klastrava. Six planes, I believe. You know the country?"

"Never heard of it."

"I'm not surprised. It's one of the smallest of the Slavic nations, north of Czechoslovakia. For all I know it was a part of Poland at one time; most of those countries were. The point is, it's a nation on the other side of the iron curtain, so of course we were somewhat startled to get this order from them. The satellite nations are encouraged to deal with the Soviet Union, you know."

"No news reports," Parker answered. "Just tell the story."

"I'm trying to give you the background."

Harrow was beginning to get petulant. Parker shrugged. Over on the bed, Bett was smiling dreamily at the ceiling.

"It's turned out," said Harrow, plunging on with his story, "that this was one of the de-Stalinization periods and Klastrava was taking advantage of the milder climate to do some of its purchasing in the more competitively priced Western market. Needless to say, we never sold them any more planes, but in the process of that sale I met a gentleman named Kapor, from the Klastravian embassy. What Kapor's normal duties are I don't know, but at the time he was handling the negotiations for the sale of the planes. I met him, as I say, and we discovered we had quite a bit in common—"

This set the daughter to laughing again, and Harrow glared at her. Then, before Parker could say anything to hurry him along, he went quickly back to his story. "At any rate, he was a house guest in my home two or three times, and once or twice when I was in Washington he invited me to stay with him. And it turned out that he too has a small collection of statuary, but of no particular value. However, his collection did include an alabaster figure of a weeping monk, approximately sixteen inches high."

Harrow smiled broadly, and rubbed his hands together. "I suspected what it must be at once, and learned that Kapor had no idea that it was anything more than an interesting piece of early-fifteenth-century statuary. I also discovered where he'd bought it. I made discreet inquiries, and gradually pieced together this little monk's history, working backward, or course, to its original home in Dijon."

"I don't need all that," Parker interrupted. Harrow seemed ready to play the romantic all week.

"Let him go, Chuck," Bett said. "He's just bubbling over to tell you all about it."

"The information cost me quite a bit," Harrow added defensively. "At one point, I even had to hire a French private investigator to check on a piece of information for me."

Parker shrugged.

"At any rate," said Harrow, hurrying now in an attempt to keep Parker from interrupting, "this particular statue was one of those looted in 1795, when revolutionaries desecrated the tomb. Who stole it I have no idea, but it did turn up in Quebec as a result of the Rebellion of 1837. Economic reprisals against one Jacques Rommelle, a follower of Louis Joseph Papineau, forced him to sell most of his possessions and move to Nova Scotia. Among the household goods sold was this small alabaster statuette. Rommelle had a knack for aligning himself with the wrong people. He'd left France for Canada in 1795, primarily because he was one of the strongest supporters of Robespierre. It's possible Rommelle personally stole the statue from Dijon, but unlikely, because he'd lived most of his life in Rennes, which is in Brittany, on the other side of France. I think it more likely that the original looter was killed during the Terror, and that Rommelle was the second owner."

He paused, cleared his throat, rubbed his hands together briskly, and smiled. "There's such a fascination in this," he said. "At any rate, Rommelle sold the statue in 1838, to a dealer named Smythe. Smythe didn't manage to resell it, and when he died in 1852, his business was inherited by a grandson who had emigrated to the United States and was at the time living in Atlanta. The grandson sold most of what he'd inherited but he did hold on to a few items he liked, among them the statue of the weeping monk, but it was stolen by a Captain Goodebloode, a Union cavalry officer in 1864, when General Sherman's army captured the city. Captain Goodebloode brought the statue to Boston, where it remained in the family till 1932, when the Goodebloode finances were depleted by the depression, and the contents of the ancestral house were sold at auction. A Miss Cannel purchased the statue in Boston and brought it home to Wittburg, a small town in upstate New York, where, for some reason best known to herself, she was attempting to set up a museum. If she'd had the wit to hire a professional curator, of course, the game would have been up right then, but this was a one-woman museum, and Miss Cannel apparently had more money than sense. At any rate, the statue went into the museum and when Miss Cannel died in 1953, the entire contents of the museum were sold to various dealers. One of them, in 1955, sold the statuette to Lepas Kapor. Finis."

Harrow looked back and forth from Parker to his daughter, beaming and happy. "A fascinating history," he said, dwelling on the words, "a fascinating history. A bloody revolution, a somewhat less bloody rebellion, a civil war, an economic crash—all have touched this small statue and influenced its destiny. It has traveled from France to Canada to Atlanta to Boston and to a provincial upstate New York town. Now it is in Washington. It has been stolen at least twice, and possibly three times, and now it is to be stolen again. A fascinating, fascinating history."

"Yeah," said Parker. He lit a cigarette and threw the match toward an ashtray. "The point is, you want me to get it for you."

"Exactly. I will give you, of course, full particulars—"

"What's in it for me?"

"What? Oh." Harrow looked puzzled for a second, but now he smiled radiantly. "Of course, you expect to be paid. You'll get the gun, for one thing, and a certain sum of money."

"What sum?"

Harrow sucked on his cheek, studying Parker's face. Finally, he said, "Five thousand dollars. In cash."

"No."

Harrow raised his eyebrows. "No? Mr. Willis, I consider the gun to be the major item of payment. Any cash would be in the nature of a bonus."

"Fifty thousand," Parker said.

"Good God! You aren't serious?"

Parker shrugged, and waited.

"Mr. Willis, I could *buy* the statuette for little more than that. I've told you, the present owner has no idea—"

"You can't buy it at all," Parker said, "or you would."

"Well." Harrow pursed his lips, glanced with an aggrieved look at his daughter, sucked on his cheek again, drummed his fingers on the book in his lap. "I'll go to ten thousand, Mr. Willis. Absolutely my top offer. Believe me, the statuette is worth no more than that to me."

"I'm not bargaining," Parker replied. "Fifty thousand or get out."

"And shall we go to the police, Mr. Willis? Shall we go to the police?"

Parker got to his feet, went over to the closet, and took out a suitcase. He opened it on the bed and turned to the dresser.

Harrow said, "Very well. Twenty-five. Half now, and the balance when you get the statuette."

Parker opened the top dresser drawer and began transferring shirts to the suitcase.

Harrow watched him a minute longer, and Bett watched them both. The father was frowning, the daughter smiling.

"Thirty-five."

Parker started on the second drawer.

"Damn it, man, we have the gun!"

Bett said, "Give up, Dad, he won't change his mind."

"Ridiculous," Harrow said. "Absurd. We have him over a barrel." He frowned in petulance at Parker. "All right. All right, stop that asinine packing, you're not fooling anyone."

Parker started on the third drawer.

"I said you could stop packing. Fifty thousand. Agreed."

Parker paused. "In advance," he said. "The fifty thousand now, the gun after I get the statue."

"Half now."

"I told you I don't bargain."

Harrow shook his head angrily. "All right. The money now, the gun afterward."

Parker left the suitcase and went back to the chair by the writing table. "All right," he said. "Come over here. Bring your chair. I want this Kapor's address. You've been in his house, I want as detailed a ground plan as you can give me. I want to know what room the statue is kept in, and if he's got more than one there I want a detailed description of the one I'm after. I want to know how many people are in the household, and what you know about the habits of each of them."

It took a while. Harrow wasn't an observant man, and his memory had to be prodded every step of the way. It took half an hour to get even an incomplete ground plan, with half the interior still terra incognita. As for the people living there, there was Lepas Kapor himself, and some servants. Harrow didn't know how many, or if any of them lived in. Kapor was unmarried, but Harrow thought that occasionally a woman stayed in the house overnight.

When Parker finally had everything from Harrow he was likely to get, Harrow was put on the send for the fifty thousand. Bett wanted to stick around for bed games, but Parker wasn't in the mood. He was never in the mood before a job, always in the mood right after.

After they'd gone, Parker went down to the bar and got Handy. Together they went over the ground plan and the sketchy information they had, and the next day, after Harrow had turned over the attaché case full of cash and Parker had checked it in the hotel safe, they took off for Washington.

Kapor lived in a sprawling colonial brick house with white trim off Garfield, four blocks from the Klastrava embassy. A five-foot hedge surrounded the property. The two-car garage was behind the house, like an afterthought. A gravel driveway led in from the street through a break in the hedge, made a left turn at the front door, and then continued on around to the garage.

Parker and Handy took turns three days and nights

watching the house, and by then they'd filled in some of the holes in Harrow's information.

There were five servants, but only one slept in. The chauffeur did not sleep in, nor did the gardener-handyman, the cook, or the maid. The butler-valet-bodyguard did sleep in. His room was on the second floor front, right corner. Kapor's room was in the back somewhere.

The house was not in an isolated neighborhood. Also, because it held an important man attached to the embassy of a country generally considered unfriendly to the United States, it was given unusually complete police surveillance. Prowl cars passed at frequent and erratic intervals day and night. There was also the possibility that the FBI or some other government agency was watching the house. It didn't look like an easy house to break into undisturbed.

Handy suggested the old tried-and-true maid ploy. Meet the maid, gain her confidence, and eventually get a chance to make an impression of the keys in her purse. With the keys, a bold frontal attack—walk straight up to the door at a relatively early hour of the night, unlock it, and go on in.

Because it was Handy's idea, and because he had a more pleasant personality, he went after the maid. He was in his early forties, tall and strong-faced, like a lean Vermont sheriff. The maid, Clara Stoper, was about

thirty and good-looking in a harsh sort of way. She spent
her Monday and Thursday nights in a bar on Wisconsin
Avenue, and it was there that Handy made the meet.
That was a week ago, and tonight he'd been going to her
apartment, where he was sure he would be able to get his
hands on the keys. She'd already given him a ten-thirty
deadline, so he'd told Parker he'd be back by eleven. But
eleven o'clock had passed and he hadn't shown up, and
then the two amateur bums had come up the fire escape
and gradually all hell had broken loose. So if Harrow had
sent this second group after that goddamn statue, Harrow was in trouble.

TWO

1

Parker left the truck a block from the bungalow, and said to Handy, "Can you keep him tight?"

"No trouble." Handy was sitting up now, and looked in better shape. He held the .380 loosely in his lap, his eye on Pliers. "He won't go anywhere."

"You guys are wasting your time," Pliers said. He looked surly and belligerent, but not very tough.

Parker got out of the truck and walked to the bungalow. It was still dark. All the houses around here were dark, and even the street lights seemed dimmed, because of the trees along the sidewalks, which cut off some of the light. Parker was the only thing moving on either sidewalk and there were no cars in sight.

There was a driveway next to the bungalow, but no garage. The driveway was just a double dirt track. Parker used it to go around to the rear. The kitchen door was locked, but it jimmied quickly and quietly. Parker stepped inside.

The house had four rooms. Living room, kitchen, two bedrooms, and a bath. Without turning on any lights, Parker moved through them and found them all empty. He went out the front door and walked back to the truck. He started it and drove to the bungalow, up the driveway, and around to the back yard. "Hold him a minute more," he said to Handy, and got out of the truck again. He went into the house and turned on the kitchen light. Enough light spilled out the rear window so he could switch off the truck lights.

Handy could walk now, but stiffly. The three of them went into the bungalow, and while Handy covered Pliers with the .380, Parker frisked him. Back at the garage he'd only gone over him for hardware; now he was emptying everything out of the man's pockets. Under the white coverall Pliers was wearing brown slacks and a green flannel shirt.

His goods gradually stacked up on the kitchen table. A wallet, a pack of Marlboros in the box, a Zippo lighter with some sort of Army insignia on one side, a pair of pliers with electrician's tape on the handles, a screwdriver, a switchblade knife, a small flat black address book, an inhaler, and a tin packet of aspirin. The wallet contained thirty-three dollars, two pictures of a girl in a bathing suit, a picture of Pliers himself in a bathing suit, and a lot of cards—Army discharge, driver's license, chauffeur's license, membership card in a Teamsters local, membership card in a gym—all made out to Walter Ambridge of Baltimore.

Finished with the wallet, Parker dropped it on the table. "All right, Wally, sit down."

"I'm called Walter." Pliers said it truculently, and he didn't sit down.

Parker hit him just above the belt. The wind whooshed out of him and he sagged. Parker pushed his shoulder slightly, to guide him, and he sat down. Handy was leaning against the refrigerator, still casually holding the .380.

Parker sat down in the other kitchen chair and rested his hands on the table. "All right, Wally," he said. "Who's Menlo?"

"Up yours."

Parker shook his head and picked up the pliers. He extended them toward Handy. "Take off his left thumbnail."

Ambridge came out of the chair roaring. They had to hit him hard enough to stun him before they could get him to sit down again. Parker waited until comprehension came back into Ambridge's eyes, and then he said, "Do we have to tie you up in the chair, Wally? Do we have to hurt you? I've been doing nothing but ask questions all night long. I don't like that. You answer in a hurry, Wally."

Ambridge glared harder than ever, to cover the fact he was frightened. He said, "You birds are in trouble, you know that? You didn't get cleared or nothing."

"Cleared? What the hell are you talking about?"

"With the Outfit, Goddamn it. You don't make any play around here without you clear it with the Outfit first. What the hell are you, amateurs?"

"Well, I'll be damned," said Parker. He knew what Ambridge was talking about, but he was surprised. He knew the Outfit—it was what the syndicate was calling itself that year—didn't like action in its territories without its approval, and he knew there were people in his line of work who never took on a job without letting the Outfit know about it first. But Parker himself would never work on a job that had been tipped to the Outfit, and he didn't know why anybody else did. The Outfit always wanted a piece, 5 or 10 per cent, for giving its permission, and permission was all it ever gave. Whatever local fix the Outfit had was no good for the transients if their deal went sour.

"So Menlo cleared this job with the Outfit. Which are you with, Menlo or the syndicate?"

"Outfit. I'm with the Outfit, on loan. Menlo didn't have no sidemen of his own."

Handy said, "He still doesn't have any worth a damn.

These guys had me for three hours and didn't get me to say one word."

"Nobody knew you had a partner." Ambridge sounded resentful, as though Handy hadn't played fair.

"Now we get to the question again," Parker said. He picked up the pliers and held them loosely in both hands. "Who is Menlo, and what's he after?"

"It don't make no difference," Ambridge said. "I can tell you and it don't make no difference at all. You guys have had it anyway. You ought to know better. You can't buck the Outfit."

Handy laughed then, because Parker had bucked the Outfit twice in the last year and hadn't done too badly either time. And when it came to operating without Outfit permission, Parker and Handy and most of the people they knew had been doing it for years.

Ambridge looked at Handy the way a patriot looks at somebody who forgets to take off his hat when the flag goes by. "You'll get yours," he said.

"Quit stalling," Parker replied.

Ambridge shrugged. "I'll tell you. It don't make no difference. This guy Menlo came around—" He looked suddenly startled, and stared at their faces. "Wait a minute," he said. "Are you guys Commies?"

Handy laughed again. "Not us, bo. We're capitalists from way back."

"Who is Menlo?" Parker was getting tired asking the same question and he was holding the pliers tighter now.

"Menlo's a defector." Ambridge said it the way a man says a good word he just recently learned. "He's from one of the Commie countries. They sent him over here to do a job for them, but he's copping out. He says this Kapor's heavy, and it's all got to be in the house, so we're taking it away from him."

"How heavy?"

"Maybe a hundred G."

Handy whistled low, but Parker said, "Crap. In cash? Where'd he get all that?"

"Don't ask me. This Menlo made a contract and talked to Mc—talked to the boss here, and the boss figured it's worth the chance for a fifty-fifty split. Menlo's got the goods, the Outfit's got the manpower. It don't make no difference, what I tell you; you can't buck the Outfit."

Maybe if he said it often enough, about his talking not making a difference, he'd start to believe it himself. Better than believing he'd been scared into it with nothing but threats.

Which meant he was probably telling the truth. The fat man, Menlo, had convinced the Outfit that Kapor's house was full of money. But where was an embassy aide from a small and unfriendly country likely to pick up a hundred thousand dollars? Either Menlo was pulling a fast one, giving the Outfit a tale in return for some muscle, or there was more to this Kapor than Harrow knew about.

The next one to see was Menlo. Parker asked, "Where's Menlo now?"

Ambridge shook his head. "I don't know. He's got the wind up, on account of you guys. He was going to stick at Clara's place, but he won't be there now."

"Don't get cute, Wally. You were supposed to get in touch with him after Handy talked. Where?"

"He didn't say. That's the straight goods, I swear to God. He just called us here and said take that guy to the garage, that he'd get in touch with us later."

Handy shifted his position against the refrigerator. "He'll be going deep now. We left the other two breathing back there."

"That's all right. Wally knows where he'd go."

"How the hell would I know?"

"He'll go where the rest of you can find him. He wants his muscle close to him. Where is it, Wally?"

"I don't know. That's the straight—"

Parker lifted the pliers again. "First we tie you," he said. "Then we take your fingernails off. Then we take your teeth out."

"What you want from me? I don't know where he is." Ambridge was sweating now, his forehead slick under the fluorescent light. "I been telling you what you want, what the hell do you think?"

"I think you're afraid of somebody finding out you let us know where to find Menlo. I think you're afraid of these pliers too. Which you afraid of most, Wally?"

"I don't *know* where he is!"

Parker turned his head to Handy. "Take a look in the drawers. People usually keep twine around. We'll have to tie him down this time."

"Wait—wait a second. Wait now, just wait a second." Ambridge was a big man, but he was fluttering now like a little man. "I mean, maybe I—"

"Don't make up any addresses, Wally. You'll give us the address and we'll keep you on ice here till we check it out, and if Menlo isn't there we'll come back and talk to you again."

"I can't be *sure* he's there! For Christ's sake, maybe he—"

"Take a chance."

"Well . . ." Ambridge wiped his palm across his forehead, and it came away wet. He looked at his wet hand with a sort of dull surprise. "I'm a coward. I'm nothing but a coward."

Handy took pity on him. "The information didn't come from you. It'll never get back to your boss."

"What good am I?" Ambridge asked himself.

It was dangerous. They'd had to push him, but there was always the chance with somebody like Ambridge, a bluffer, that you'd push him too hard and he'd be forced to look at himself and see the truth. You take a coward, and you force him to look at himself and see that he *is* a coward, he's liable all of a sudden to not give a damn anymore, to get fatalistic and despairing. If he gets to that point, all of a sudden nothing will work on him anymore, no threats no punishment. He'll just sit there and take it, thinking he deserves it anyway, thinking he's dead anyway so what difference does it make?

Ambridge was on the edge of that, and Parker could see it. A few more seconds, and Ambridge would be unreachable. Parker reached out and slapped him across the face, open-handed, a contemptuous slap, and said with scorn, "Hurry it up, punk. You're wasting my time."

It was enough. The slap didn't hurt, but it stung. So did the words, and the tone behind them. It was enough to snap Ambridge out of his introspection. He threw up the old defenses again, came back with the bluff as strong as ever. He glared at Parker and started up out of the chair. Parker and Handy had to work a little to get him to sit down again, then Parker said, "You started to give us the address. Now give."

It was the old Ambridge who answered. "You think it makes any difference? You think you can just walk in and take him? You think he's alone? You go after him and you're both dead."

"Let us worry about that."

"You'll worry about it. There's a house in Bethesda, on

Bradley Boulevard. Menlo's got the borrow of it from the Outfit till the job's done. We were supposed to call him there after we found out what your partner was up to. Go on out there, get your heads blown off. I only wish I could be there to watch."

They had him write the address down, and then they tied him and left him in a closet. They never did remember to go back.

2

On that block was a row of two-family houses, built before the war. The one they wanted was on the corner. What the Outfit used it for normally they didn't know, but right now Menlo was living in the downstairs flat, and the upstairs flat, according to Ambridge, was empty.

They'd stopped off on the way to get rid of the truck and pick up their own car, where Handy had left it earlier in the evening. The car was a Pontiac, two years old. It was hot, but not on the East coast, and the papers on it were a good imitation of the real thing.

Handy was driving, and a block from the address he took his foot off the accelerator. The car slowed. There were taillights ahead. A car was double-parked in front of the house they wanted, lights on and motor running.

"Go on past," Parker said. "Then around the block."

Parker looked the car over on the way by. It was a

black Continental. The man at the wheel wore a chauffeur's cap and was reading the *Star*. The car carried New York plates, and they started DPL. Diplomat. Beyond the car was the house, the ground floor all lit up, the upper story dark.

It was almost three o'clock in the morning. The Continental out front with diplomat plates at three in the morning wasn't a good sign. Parker said, "Hurry around the block. Park on the cross street."

"I'm ahead of you," Handy answer. "What did that guy say Menlo was? A defector?"

"Yeah."

They left the Pontiac half a block from Bradley, on the side street that flanked the house they wanted. This way they could get to the back door without tipping the chauffeur in the Continental.

There was a white picket fence separating the back yard from the sidewalk, with a white picket gate. The gate opened with no trouble and no squeaking, and they went across the slate walk to the stoop and up onto the back porch. The kitchen door stood wide open, and the storm door was closed but not locked. The kitchen was empty, but casting bright, wide swatches of light out through the window and doorway.

Handy's touch with doors was the lightest. The storm door never made a sound. They stood on linoleum with a black-and-white diamond design, and listened. The re-

frigerator hummed, and on a different note the circular
fluorescent light in the ceiling also hummed. The rest of
the house was silent. Bright and silent.

An open door to the right led to a bedroom, but with
no bed in it. The ceiling light was on—two seventy-five-
watt-bulbs unshielded—and in the glare the bedroom
was a bleak cubicle full of unmarked cardboard cartons,
stacked along the walls. The venetian blinds were down
across both windows.

A hall led off the kitchen. Midway along it was a brace
of doorways facing each other. The one on the left opened
onto the bathroom, gleaming with white tile and white
porcelain and white enamel, with a brightly burning
white fluorescent tube over the mirror above the sink.
The doorway on the right led to another bedroom, this
one containing a bed. This too was garishly lit, and
looked like a whore's crib. A double bed dominated the
room, covered by a cheap tan spread, and without pillows. A scarred dresser stood on the opposite wall, and
the bed was flanked on one side by a black kitchen chair
and on the other by a small wooden table containing
nothing but a chipped ashtray.

At the end of the hall was a dining room, lit by a rococo ceiling fixture of rose-tinted glass. The cream-and-
tan wallpaper was a faded pattern of ivy and Grecian
columns. Centered beneath the light was a poker table,
round and covered with green felt, with eight wells

around the outer edge for the players' money and drinks. Eight chairs crouched around the table, on a faded Oriental rug. There was no other furniture in the room.

The third bedroom, off the dining room, was apparently the one Menlo was using, for there was clothing draped on the chair, hairbrush and cufflinks and other things on the dresser, and an expensive-looking alarm clock on the night table.

A wide archway led from dining room to living room, which was furnished in an old-fashioned way, in dark colors and heavy overstuffed furniture.

Every light in the house was on, and the Continental still waited out front, though all the rooms were empty.

Handy caught Parker's eye, and pointed at the floor. Parker nodded. Still moving cautiously and silently, they went back to the kitchen. The first door they tried opened onto the pantry, but the second showed cellar stairs angling away to the left. Light came up from below, and the sound of someone talking, softly and conversationally. And there was another sound, a steady scraping and chuffing, slow and rhythmic.

Handy already had the .380 out. Parker unlimbered the Terrier, and led the way down. The stairs angled sharply to the left, and then went straight down the rest of the way, toward the rear wall of the house, so that most of the basement was behind Parker as he came down. He came halfway, then crouching on the stairs, ducked his head under the banister and looked back at the rest of the cellar.

Three hundred-watt bulbs were spaced along under the I-beam that ran down the middle of the ceiling. All were unshielded, and all were lit, throwing the dirt-floored cellar in stark, almost shadowless, relief. An old coal furnace hulked on one side, with its squat oil converter crouched in front of it. Several barrels of trash were standing alongside two deep metal sinks.

Down at the other end, the fat man was digging his own grave, while three men surrounded him, watching. Two of the three stood silently, pistols in their hands. The third had brought a kitchen chair down with him— or had someone bring it down for him—and was sitting comfortably on it, his back to Parker. He seemed nattily dressed, and he was the one doing the talking, a steady soft flow of easy conversation, a monologue almost, in a language Parker didn't recognize. It was guttural, but not in a Germanic way.

Handy had seen too. He grinned and motioned for them to go back upstairs, but Parker shook his head. Handy looked puzzled and leaned forward to whisper. "They're getting rid of the competition. Why not let them?"

Parker whispered back, "If there's more than a statue in Kapor's house, I want to know what it is and where to find it. The fat man knows."

Handy shrugged. "I'll take the one on the left."

They leaned out on different sides of the staircase, showing only their heads and gun hands. The shots roared out in that confined space like cauvette blowing up.

Before the two gunmen had hit the ground, the talkative one was out his chair, spinning around, a flat white automatic coming out from under his coat. Parker and Handy both fired again, and the automatic sailed into the air as he toppled backward into the grave Menlo had only half dug.

Menlo, again moving faster than any fat man should, threw himself off to the side and rolled over against the side wall. But when there weren't any more shots, he got to his feet cautiously. His white shirt was a sweaty, dirty mess, his black trousers rumpled and baggy. He was barefoot, and his face and hands were also covered with dirt. He stood peering toward the stairs until Parker and Handy moved toward him, and then suddenly he smiled. "Ah!" he said. "How glad I am I did not pause to kill you at poor Clara's."

"Let's go," Parker said.

"So soon? But I have not yet expressed my appreciation. You have saved my life!"

"We'll talk later, what do you say?" Handy added.

Menlo looked around at the three scattered bodies.

"There is much in what you say," he said. "Have you dealt with the chauffeur?"

"We won't have to. Come on."

"Most certainly."

Parker went first, and then Menlo, with Handy last. They filed upstairs to the kitchen, and as Parker reached for the storm door, Menlo said, "Please! Would you take me away in such a condition?"

"You can wash up later," Handy said.

"But my shoes! My coat! My personal possessions!"

"Come on," said Parker.

"Let him get his stuff," Handy said. "What the hell?"

"You watch him, then."

"Sure."

Parker waited in the kitchen. They were gone two minutes by the kitchen clock, and when they came back Menlo was wearing shoes and a topcoat. The topcoat was too tight for him, making him look like somebody on a Russian reviewing stand. He was carrying a black attaché case covered with good leather.

Parker pointed at it. "What's in there?"

"I checked it," Handy said. "Just clothes and a flask."

"And a toothbrush," Menlo added. His face was still dirty, and when he smiled he looked like the fat boy in a silent movie comedy. "I am most proud of my teeth."

"Let's go."

They went out the back way and down the block to

their car. Parker got behind the wheel, and Handy and Menlo sat in back. "Where do we go from here?" Handy asked.

"Back to the hotel."

"What if they come looking there again?"

Parker shook his head. "The only ones who looked were Menlo's people. And Menlo doesn't have people any more. Do you, Menlo?"

Menlo smiled again, with mock wistfulness, and spread dirty hands. "Only you," he replied. "My two newly found friends."

Parker started the car. When they crossed the intersection, the Continental was still waiting out front—the lights on, the motor running, the chauffeur deeply immersed in the *Star*.

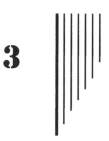

3

Bett Harrow stretched lazily and got up off the bed. "It's about time you came home. Three-thirty in the morning. Who are these nice people? And what happened to that man's face?"

Parker said, "Get the hell out of here."

"Daddy sent me for a progress report, sweetie. All that money spent and not one word from you. He got nervous. Fifty thousand dollars is fifty thousand dollars."

"An axiom, my dear," said Menlo, smiling and advancing, his hand extended. "You have stated what is possibly the ultimate truth. I am Auguste Menlo, yours to command." She gave him her hand, smiling, and he bent low over it, kissing it.

"Sit down, fat man, and shut your face," Parker said. "Bett, tell your father I'll see him when I'm done. Now get out of here."

Menlo shrugged prettily, smiling his quixotic smile. He had a way of moving as though he were making fun of his weight. "I must obey," he said to Bett. "Your friend has just saved my life. The least I owe him is obedience."

He sat down on the chair with the broken arm, crossed his ankles, and discovered the damage. "I had expected better from American hotels," he said, frowning.

Bett strolled casually toward the door, detouring slightly to cross close to Parker. "I know you must have important things to discuss," she said. "We can talk later." She moistened her lips, and her eyes gleamed. "My room is just down the hall. Five-twelve. It was the closest I could get to you, Parker. Don't take too long. You never know what I might do if you upset me." She went on out.

Menlo kissed his fingertips in appreciation, and made a small salute toward the closed door. "A beautiful creature," he said. "A magnificent woman."

Parker lit a cigarette and pulled a chair over close to Menlo. "That isn't what we'll talk about."

"No, of course. I quite understand."

"That's good."

"Might I have a cigarette?"

Handy came over and gave him one, and a light to go with it. Menlo made a production out of how much he liked the cigarette, blowing smoke at the ceiling. "Ah! One of the few things for which America will be remembered. If you have ever smoked European cigarettes, you must know what I mean."

Handy was still standing next to Menlo. He leaned down now, and said, "Listen to me, friend. My partner's a very impatient man. Besides, he's sore about her being here. You keep horsing around, he'll take it out on you."

"I am most sorry." Menlo sat forward at once, uncrossing his ankles, sitting at attention, an expression of concern on his face. "It is my way, Mr.—"

"Parker."

"Parker. Yes. It is only my way, Mr. Parker. I mean no offense by it, I assure you. I will come most directly to the point."

"That's good," Parker said.

Menlo smiled. "Yes, that's good. And the point, Mr. Parker, is: Why did you save my life?" He looked brightly from Parker to Handy, and back again. "Eh? Isn't that interesting? Why did you save my life?"

Handy said, "Go a little faster, huh? Quit repeating yourself."

"Yes, of course. But the question, you see, the question has many aspects. It is prismatic. With such a question, one can see around corners. With such a question, one can receive many other answers. For example—I am trying to hurry, I most honestly am—for instance, when I became aware of you, Mr. Castle—Mr. Castle?"

Handy shrugged. "It'll do."

"Of course. When I became aware of you, I said to myself, is this coincidence? Could you possibly be interested in the same goal toward which *I* was directing myself? Thus I had you summoned for questioning, and thus the additional events which have transpired. But now you and Mr. Parker have saved my life, and all at once the answer is clear. Your goal is *not* the same as mine. Or at least it was not, until tonight. Did you save my life for humanitarian reasons? Hardly. There could be only one other reason. To keep me alive until such time as you would know what I already know. Which means that for all your threatening statements and glowering expressions, you cannot risk having me dead."

"Nobody said anything about having you dead," Parker said.

"I must explain," said Menlo. He smiled again, pleased with himself. "Becuase of my occupation these past fifteen years, I have been equipped for instant self-annihilation. One of my teeth is false; it contains a capsule. Should I bite down hard in a certain way—a rather awkward way, to avoid doing so unintentionally—I would break that capsule. Should that happen, my breath would smell pleasingly of almonds, and I would very soon be dead. That is what Spannick was talking to me about tonight, in the cellar, while I was digging my own grave. He was suggesting to me that I save the state the price of a bullet. But where there is life, as your proverb so succinctly puts it, there is hope. In this case, well-founded hope." He smiled some more. His teeth gleamed.

"If we try to hurry you," Parker said, "you'll kill yourself. Is that it?"

"If you try to hurry me in too physical and violent a fashion, yes. I have an extremely low pain threshold. The price of high intelligence and self-indulgence. Ah, this is really a most excellent cigarette." Menlo leaned back again in the chair, and recrossed his ankles. "I will now tell you the facts. In my own way. And at my own rate of speed. If you find yourself becoming too impatient, Mr. Parker, you might perhaps spend your time instead with that charming lady who was earlier here. Your associate could rapidly and succinctly tell you the highlights later."

Parker shook his head, got to his feet, and went over to lie down on the bed. The world was full of people who never did anything but talk. "Any time you feel like it," he said.

"You are most gracious." Menlo took a deep breath, thought for a second to organize his thoughts, and began talking. "Our mutual target, Lepas Kapor, has for the past eight years been one of our most important liaison agents with our espionage network in this country. As an aide at the embassy of such a small and insignificant nation as Klastrava, he was far less likely to come under the scrutiny and suspicion of American counterintelligence. His duties have been twofold. First, he transmits information from the network to the Soviet Union. Second, he furnishes funds to pay for the network's continued existence, to cover the cost of bribes and payoffs and so on. Just recently, we discovered that Kapor has systematically been cheating us ever since getting this assignment. His method is simplicity itself. Say a particular document cost one thousand dollars to obtain. In his report he would state that it cost fifteen hundred dollars, and the overage he would merely transfer to his own pockets. How much he has accrued for himself in this way we can only guess, but the estimate is that he has stolen more than ten thousand dollars a year for eight years. Perhaps in all, one hundred thousand dollars."

Menlo looked smilingly at Handy, and then at Parker. "Interesting? Yes. Of course it is. And even more interesting is the question, what has he done with this money? Has he spent it? Hardly. An obscure aide in an obscure embassy? If he were to live beyond his means, it would be noticed at once. Shall he bank it? Considering the political orientation of Klastrava and the passion for voluminous records among bankers, this too seems hardly the answer. Nor can he invest it. He can, in fact, do nothing with it so long as he remains in his present post. He can only secrete it, somewhere in his own house, against the day when he will suddenly disappear. He intends to retire, of course, in some out-of-the-way place. South America perhaps, or Mexico. Or it is entirely possible that he will remain in the United States, in Vermont or Oregon or Nebraska. A man with a hundred thousand dollars can arrange to disappear almost anywhere."

Handy interrupted. "How do you know for sure it's in cash, and that it's in his house? Maybe he's got it buried out in the country someplace."

"Ah, wait. I'm coming to that. Please be patient."

Parker sat up and lit a fresh cigarette. For half of a hundred thousand dollars, he could make himself be patient.

"Now comes my own entry into the story," Menlo continued. "I am, in a way, a policeman. Not precisely the sort you two have undoubtedly encountered at one time or another in your careers. My occupation has no true counterpart in your country, except unofficially, among the members of some stern-jawed American society or the more belligerent American Legion posts. My duties are, in a way, religious, with an analogy drawn from the Spanish Inquisition. I am an inquisitor, a seeker of heretics, of those whose heresies are against the state. It was felt that a man of my background and unquestioned loyalty would be best suited to the task of punishing Lepas Kapor and of regaining the embezzled funds. It was decided not to trust this delicate task to our espionage organization; news of this impending doom might perhaps somehow reach the ears of our suspect. And so, for the first time in my life, I left my native land—armed with a valid passport and a map to a cache containing one hundred thousand American dollars!"

Menlo threw his head back and laughed, a full booming laugh of delight. "It was *wonderful!* The opportunity of a lifetime!" Then his laughter subsided and he leaned forward confidentially. "Do you know what my pension would be, were I to live to the retirement age of sixty-seven? In American money, it would be—let me see—approximately five hundred and thirty dollars a year. And yet they expected me to find this hidden cache of *one hundred thousand dollars* in American money, and *bring it back!*"

He shook his head. "I am not a fool. My dear friends, you will discover that about me. I am most shockingly overweight, and far too self-indulgent, but you will find that I am not a fool."

"So you figured to take the money and run?" Handy asked.

"Would you not? Of course. Let me tell you what I did. Laboriously, I managed to contact members of the American underworld. I was then introduced to an organization which calls itself the Outfit. It claims to exert total control over crime within the areas of its control but having met you two, it is only natural that I begin to doubt this claim. Nevertheless, I met with these people, and I discussed the situation with them. It was agreed that they would furnish me assistants and protection from local law-enforcement agencies, and—what do they call that? Protection from local law-enforcement agencies."

"The fix," Handy said.

"Yes! The fix is in. That's what it was. I was delighted with the phrase. The French are so pleased with their criminal argot, but I assure you the Americans in this regard have nothing to be ashamed of. The fix is in."

"Get on with it," Parker said.

"You have no interest in your native idiom? A pity. As I was saying, I met with these people, and we came to a financial agreement which of course I had no intention of honoring. And thus the operation was set in motion. We moved most cautiously, I assure you, not wanting to flush our bird prematurely from the nest. What had led to the discovery of Kapor's ingeniousness in the first place were some small slight indications that he might be planning to make a sudden move, to defect or disappear. There is a large amount of money due to pass through his hands very shortly, and we were convinced he was waiting only for its arrival before making his own departure. Unavoidable delays have kept that money from reaching him thus far, so he still rests upon his perch, awaiting my pleasure."

"How close were you?" Parker asked.

"We had intended to enter the house this coming Friday. Kapor will be at an official dinner most of the evening, and we intended to be in the house already upon his return."

Menlo shifted his bulk in the chair and looked with an innocent smile at Parker. "This plan could still be effected," he went on. "Without the minions of the Outfit, of course. I doubt that they were ever really happy with the operation. They disliked the thought of being connected even indirectly with international politics, but the harvest was too tempting to be missed. Now, because of all the trouble you two caused tonight, they have abandoned the plan completely. Spannick informed me of this with great pleasure tonight, while watching me dig. The Outfit recalled those who had helped me, and recouped its losses by selling to Spannick the information that I had intended in my own turn to steal the money. So the Outfit is no longer concerned with Kapor. Spannick is dead, and if I know that egotistical idiot, he would not have made any report on me until he had already done me in. He always preferred telling his superiors about a problem only after he had already solved it. Which means that Kapor has been left to us."

Parker studied the fat man's face. "Us?"

"But of course. You have business of your own with Kapor, though I confess I cannot imagine what it is. In addition, you would no doubt like to share in that hundred thousand dollars. I need assistance, which you can give me. You need to know the location of the money, which I can give you."

"You know where it is?"

"The exact spot. I must say, it is exceedingly well hidden. I hardly think you could find it without me."

"How come you know where it is?" Handy asked.

"Clara told me. She had weeks to look for it, and eventually she found it. Poor Clara."

Menlo smiled again, his ingenuous smile. "I forgot to tell you. I returned to Clara's apartment tonight, Mr. Parker, after you had left. You had mistreated the poor girl most terribly. The only humane thing I could do was end her misery."

He beamed.

Parker stubbed his cigarette. "I didn't ask her enough questions," he said.

"You are hardly to be blamed. You must have thought of her as only a pawn in our game. How could you know she was the key?"

"So you want to team up with us?"

"It seems most logical, does it not? My information, your experience. And we will, of course, split evenly. Half for me, half for you."

The fat man wouldn't be getting any of it, but Parker,

for appearance's sake, made a complaint. "That's no even split. A third for each of us."

Menlo spread his hands and smiled. "If you insist. I am not greedy, I assure you."

So the fat man was planning a double-cross too, Parker thought, and asked, "You still want to do it Friday?"

"That strikes me as the best time, yes. By the way, could you possibly tell me what it is that you two are concerned with in Kapor's house? That lovely girl mentioned the sum of fifty thousand dollars."

"Kapor's got a statue, supposed to be one of the lost statues from some tomb in France. A collector gave us fifty thousand to steal it from him."

"One of the mourners of Dijon?" Menlo smiled in surprise. "I have read of them, of course. How romantic! And a collector, you say? That charming girl's father, no doubt. I would most like to meet him."

"Maybe I can arrange it," Parker said.

4

Her full name was Elizabeth Ruth Harrow Conway. She was, as the fat man had said, a magnificent female, twenty-nine years old, and with honey hair made to gleam in candlelight. She had the hollow-cheeked aristocratic face that comes of generations of breeding and inbreeding, and the tall, lush, well-proportioned body of a stripper crossed with a Channel swimmer. She was rich now, and had been all her life, living currently on a combination of alimony from her ex-husband and atonement gifts from her father. She was well-sexed, with an occasional liking for self-cruelty, and she kept her hotel-room door unlocked.

Parker came in and closed the door and stood there looking at her. "Whose idea was this? Yours or your father's?"

She was in bed, with the covers up to her neck, and

two pillows under her head. She smiled languorously and stretched, her body moving lazily under the blanket. "It was mine, Chuck, don't you know that? But Daddy thinks it was his."

"Either you take off, or there's no job."

"Now, don't threaten me like that, Chuck. Be nice." She slid one arm out from under the covers and patted the bed next to her hip. "Come sit down beside me and we'll talk."

He shook his head. "Forget it."

"Be nice, Chuck," she murmured. "Be nice to me, and I'll go away first thing in the morning. If you still want me to."

That would have been a solution, but he rejected it without bothering to think about it. This was the way he always was before a job. He lived to a pattern. Immediately after a job he was a satyr, inexhaustible and insatiable. Then gradually it would taper off, and by the time the next job was in preparation he was a total celibate. When a job was being set up, he could only think of one thing. Bett's offer slid past him as though it had never been made. It simply didn't interest him.

"You'll go away first thing in the morning, or the deal's off," he said. "And you won't come back. I'll see you after I give your father the statue."

"Maybe I won't feel like it then."

He shrugged.

She was still trying to be coy and seductive, but the edges were getting ragged. "What if I decide not to be an obedient little girl, Chuck?"

"Your father's out fifty grand."

Her languorous smile all at once turned sour, and she popped to a sitting position, her face twisted in a frown of anger. The sheet and blanket fell to her waist. She was nude and her breasts were heavy but firm, and tanned as golden as the rest of her. She said, bite in her voice, "What's the matter with you, Chuck? This is little Bett, remember? We're not exactly strangers."

It was true. For most of two weeks they'd shared the same bedroom, though they'd seen each other only twice since.

"I've got other things to think about," Parker said.

"You want to be careful, Chuck," she said. Her voice was hard as a stone. "You want to be very careful with me."

"I'll see you when the job is done."

"I'm not so sure. And just a minute, don't leave yet. We've got more to talk about."

He kept his hand on the doorknob. "Such as?"

"Such as those other two men. The one that looks like you, only more pleasant, and the funny fat one. You didn't say anything to Daddy about working with anybody else."

"How I work is my business. Don't be here in the morning."

She was going to say something else; but he didn't give her a chance.

The other two were already asleep when Parker got back to his room. Menlo was staying here tonight, sleeping on the floor, and the three of them would move to another location tomorrow. Parker stepped over Menlo, stripped, and got into bed. He fell asleep the way he always did, completely and immediately.

He was a light sleeper. Normal predictable sounds—traffic outside a window, a radio playing that had been playing when he'd gone to sleep—didn't disturb him, but any unusual noise would have him completely awake at once. So when Menlo got up from the floor and crept cautiously toward the door, Parker came awake. He lay unmoving on the bed, watching Menlo through slitted eyes. Menlo took the time to pick up his suit coat and tie and shoes, but nothing else. He went out, the shoes in his hand, the coat and tie over his arm.

There was no point stopping him. Parker went back to sleep.

He awoke again when Menlo returned. The fat man was once again carrying shoes and coat and tie, but now he was carrying his shirt as well, and in the faint light from the window Parker could see that he was smiling to himself. So Bett had got what she'd come for after all. He wondered if Menlo had.

5

"**G**o," said Handy. He thumbed the stopwatch; it read just about nine o'clock.

Parker edged the Pontiac away from the curb in front of Kapor's house. Moving with the traffic, they went straight over Garfield to Massachusetts Avenue, and then turned right on Wisconsin. That took them through Georgetown and on north out of the city into Chevy Chase, and then Bethesda. It was a commercial road all the way, with more traffic than Parker liked on a getaway route, but it was the quickest, shortest way.

Menlo, sitting on the backseat like a renegade Buddha, watched with interest. At one point he said, "I still don't see why this is necessary. Kapor will hardly be in a position to notify the authorities."

Parker was busy driving, so Handy explained. "You say the Outfit's given up on this job, and maybe they did and maybe they didn't. You claim Spannick was the only one of your old crowd that knew what you were up to, and maybe he was and maybe he wasn't. We're going through the play the same night you planned, because it's a good setup. Besides, now that Clara's dead there's nobody inside to let us know when the next good time is. But we're running it an hour earlier than you figured just in case there is still somebody interested in you or Kapor's hundred grand. And we're working out the best route for the same reason."

"Then why go only so far as the motel? Why not continue on our way as rapidly as possible? We might go to Baltimore, for instance, and come to rest there."

Handy turned farther around in the seat, so he could talk full-face with Menlo. "Listen. If what we wanted was to get a confession out of Kapor, we'd let you handle it all the way. That's what you're a pro at; we'd follow anything you said. But what we're doing is breaking into Kapor's house and grabbing his goods, and that's what *we're* pros at. So you just let us do it, O.K."

"My dear friend," said Menlo, looking concerned, "please not to misjudge me. I mean no distrust of your abilities. You are most certainly professionals at your craft, and I appreciate this. It is in a spirit of curiosity only that I ask these questions. I would like to learn more." This was all said too earnestly to be sarcasm;

Menlo was perched forward on the seat, his hands pressed to his chest in a gesture of honesty.

Parker would have just told him to keep his mouth shut and watch and learn, but Handy didn't mind talking. "All right," he said, "I'll explain it to you. There's three ways to handle the getaway. You can do like you said, just take off and keep going, maybe a couple hundred miles. Or you can just go two blocks and hole up there till the heat's off. Or you can go a few miles and hole up and wait four or five hours and *then* take off and go your couple hundred miles. Now, if you do the first, take off and keep going, you're on the road all the time you're the most hot, and that's the way to get yourself picked up fast. If you hole up real close and stay there a week or two, you're right where the most cops are doing the most looking, and that's the way to get picked up six or seven days after the job, when you go out for more groceries. But if you hole up nearby for a few hours, you throw everybody off stride. If the law is after you and they've thrown up roadblocks, they stay up for a few hours and then the cops figure you either got through quick or you're holed up, and they take the roadblocks down. See what I mean? Right after the job is when they do their looking on the roads, and later is when they do their looking in town. So right after the job is when we stay in town, and later on is when we're on the roads. It's a feint, like in basketball. You *go*, but you don't go, and *then* you go."

Menlo nodded happily. "Yes, I follow. I can see where that would be the method most difficult for the authorities to counteract. But in this case, we need have no fear of authorities. Kapor will feel his loss most deeply, of course, but he will not contact the police."

"Not Kapor, no. But suppose some servant sees it first, that somebody's broken in, and calls the cops before he tells his boss? So whether Kapor likes it or not, the law will be in on it. Or maybe the Outfit is still hot for that money, and they'll show up at nine-thirty, the way you originally figured. They find out the swag is gone, the Outfit's after us. Or maybe it's your old group, friend's of Spannick's. We do it the safe way, the reliable way, and we never get jugged."

Menlo smiled with a touch of sadness. "I must say you remove the romance most utterly from all this. I had been seeing myself in quite dramatic terms. The defecting policeman, meting out poetic justice to the embezzler by depriving him of his ill-gotten gains, then disappearing again, quite forever, an enigma to all who seek him. But now I find I am merely a participant in a dreary and pedestrian series of quite normal activities— opening doors, driving automobiles, sitting in motel rooms." He shrugged and spread his hands.

Parker slowed the car. The motel was just ahead—the

Town Motel. They'd picked it because it was on the right side of the road, and because it was built in a U shape, on a slope down from the road, so that parked cars could not be seen from the street.

Parker made the turn, drove down into the court, and parked. Handy thumbed the watch and read it. "Just over eighteen minutes."

"Not good," Parker said.

"It's the fastest way," Handy told him.

They'd spent most of the afternoon trying various suburbs and motels, and this one had been the quickest by far. So now they had run it again at the same time of night they would be coming over it Friday. It was Wednesday, and they could expect a little more traffic on Friday, but they'd still done well. The traffic had been heavy, with the majority of the drivers—like the majority of all eastern drivers—spending the majority of their time in the passing lane. Parker had driven mostly in the right-hand lane, and had made better time than any other car on the road.

Still, he wasn't satisfied. "What if we holed up right at Kapor's house, until maybe two or three in the morning? Menlo, will Kapor be coming home alone?"

"Alas, no. Kapor is notoriously a party giver. A select group of friends, perhaps fifteen or twenty, will probably return with him from the dinner. This is always his habit, and I see no reason to expect that it will differ on Friday."

Parker shrugged. It wasn't good. Eighteen minutes on the road; with Friday's traffic, probably twenty or more. Their direction would be obvious before they were six blocks from Kapor's house. Twenty minutes was plenty of time to set up a block in front of them. He shook his head. "Let's go inside and study the map."

They clambered out of the car, Menlo with difficulty, and went up the stairs to their second-level rooms. Parker and Handy had a double, Menlo a single, three rooms down the hall.

In the room, Menlo settled in the most comfortable chair, while Handy stretched out on his bed. Parker got out the Washington-area map and studied it, frowning. "We could go over to a parallel street, but coming back's no good. The lights along the road out there give maximum red to the side streets. We'd just sit there, half a minute or more."

"Then we work a switch," Handy said. "Use another car on the job, and stash the Pontiac along the way."

"That's better. Adds more time, but it's better. Who knows about the Pontiac?"

Handy considered. "Nobody," he said. "Clara knew, that's all. Menlo's boys grabbed me in Clara's place." He looked over at Menlo. "Were they following us?"

"No, no. They waited at poor Clara's apartment for you to arrive."

"O.K. So the Pontiac's clean."

Parker folded the road map and put it away. He turned to Menlo. "Next question. What tools do we want?"

"I beg your pardon?"

"Tools, tools. The dough isn't just sitting out on a coffee table, is it?"

Menlo's smile was faintly surprised. "My dear friend, you most certainly don't expect me to tell you where to find it. My usefulness would then be at its end, would it not? You have been so kind as to include me only because of this one piece of information I have and you do not."

"I'm not asking you where it is. I'm asking you what do we need to get at it. Like if it's buried under concrete we need a pick, and maybe a couple caps of dynamite. Or if it's in a safe, we need a drill and a set of pullers for the combination or maybe some nitro, depending on what kind of safe it is."

"Ah, I see. The professional mind at work once again. But there is no difficulty, I assure you. No special tools will be required other than our own efficient hands."

Parker nodded. "All right. What size bag do we want? How big a bundle?"

"Well, I have not as yet seen this cash in actuality, only in my imagination. But from the manner of its secretion, let us say, I would suppose a container approximately the size of your suitcase would be more than sufficient."

"I'll get another one tomorrow, just like it." Parker got to his feet and lit a cigarette, pacing back and forth across the room. "Once more, to be sure. Kapor's leaving the house at five o'clock. The chauffeur's driving him, and will wait for him until the dinner is over. His bodyguard's going with him too. The cook will fix stuff for the party later on, but she'll be out of there by six, and so will the gardener. Kapor won't be back before ten, and maybe later. Between six and ten nobody's home."

"Most precisely."

From the bed, Handy said, "We like to be precise."

"What about this party after ten o'clock? No servants?" Parker asked.

"Oh, no. It will not be that sort of party. Morgan, Kapor's bodyguard, will serve as bartender. No other servants will be needed."

"There's no burglar alarms in the house?"

"Clara was quite certain on that point."

"All right." Parker sat down on his own bed, flicked ashes into the nearest ashtray. "So now we wait two days."

6

Handy was driving. They were working the side streets, back and forth, Handy sitting casual at the wheel and Parker beside him, studying the parked cars. Menlo was back at the motel.

It was seven-thirty Friday night, and already dark. The occasional major streets they crossed were full of slow-moving traffic, people heading downtown for a night out or uptown for a weekend out of town. The side streets were quiet, with few moving cars and only an occasional pedestrian.

They'd been looking for twenty minutes, and finally Parker said, "There it is."

Handy saw it too. He stopped the car.

Parker got out and closed the door, and Handy drove the Pontiac away. Parker crossed the street and strolled down toward the car.

97

It was a Cadillac, gleaming black, four or five years old. Being in this neighborhood, it had to be on its second owner by now, or maybe third. Still, whoever owned it kept it clean. It wouldn't look out of place turning into Kapor's driveway.

The street was empty. There were no faces in any of the house windows that Parker could see. He stopped next to the Cadillac and tried both doors. He was in luck; the rear one was unlocked. It was the rear door that people forgot most often. He hadn't needed the luck. He could have got into the Cadillac in thirty seconds even if it had been locked, but this way he didn't have to break the side vent. He opened the rear door slightly, reached around and pulled the front lock button by the front window. Then he shut the rear door, opened the front, and got in.

He lay down on the seat and took out a pencil flash. He studied the underpart of the dashboard and found he would have to remove a small, flat plate. He put the flash away, got out a small screwdriver and, working by feel, removed the three screws that held the plate in place. Then he used the flash again, for ten seconds, and that was it. He sat up, slid over behind the wheel, and took a jumper wire out of his pocket, with sticky electric tape at both ends. He unreeled part of the tape and then, working by feel once more, reached down under the dashboard and put the jumper on. The starter caught, and slipped, and caught again, and then the engine was purring. He put the automatic transmission in Drive, and pulled away.

On Wisconsin Avenue there was a movie theater, and there was a supermarket, and a blacktop parking lot between them. In the daytime the supermarket customers used the lot, and at night the movie customers used it. Parker drove there, parked the Cadillac so there was a space on his left, stalled the car, and removed the jumper wire. Then he got out and opened the hood. He stood looking down for a minute, and then went to work. It was now twenty minutes to eight.

Handy and Menlo showed up in the Pontiac on schedule, at ten minutes to eight. They parked in the slot next to the Cadillac, and got out. Parker was just finishing. He closed the hood and said, "All ready."

"Once again," Menlo said, looking at the Cadillac with distrust, "I can only reassure myself with the knowledge that you are professionals in this type of activity. The idea of driving to a robbery in an automobile just recently stolen would never have occurred to me. Having occurred to me, it would terrify me so completely I would reject it."

"This car won't be hot for a couple of hours. By then we'll be done with it," Handy said.

"I trust your judgment implicitly," Menlo assured him, "having seen you in action against those poor specimens supplied me by the Outfit. I have every confidence in you."

"That's good. Get in the car," Parker said.

"Most certainly."

Menlo got in the back again, and Parker and Handy up front. There was now a new set of wires by the steering shaft, ending in a small oblong fixture with a pushbutton. This was the new starter. Parker tested it out, and it worked fine. He backed the Cadillac out of its parking slot and drove it slowly out onto Wisconsin Avenue.

Kapor's house, when they got there, was in darkness, the way it was supposed to be. Parker spun the wheel and the Cadillac entered the driveway. The tires crunched on the gravel. The Cadillac looked right at home here as Parker tooled it around behind the house and left it in front of the garage, hidden from the street by the house.

It was eight-thirty. They were right on schedule.

There were two back doors to choose from and they picked the one that Clara had reported led to the kitchen. Handy went to work on it. He was very good with doors. It opened almost immediately.

They went in, and Parker turned on the pencil flash. From Clara, through Menlo, they now had a good ground plan of the house. His voice soft, Parker asked, "All right, Menlo. What room do we want?"

"We'll get your statuette first," Menlo said. "I have a

THE MOURNER

desire to see it. This bit of romanticism you will not de-
prive me of."

Parker shrugged. It didn't make any difference. He
crossed the kitchen and opened the door on the other
side, which led to the rear staircase, the servants' stairs.
The staircase ended on a squarish room, with a large
table along one wall. On the other side was a doorless en-
tranceway, leading to an L-shaped hall. Parker opened
the third door on the left, and because this room faced
the rear of the house, he switched on the light.

It was a long and narrow room, with a dark-red paper
covering the walls. The lighting was soft, furnished by
fluorescent tubes in troughs spaced along the upper
walls, and a rich green carpet covered the entire floor.

It resembled a room in a museum. Glass-topped cases
contained coins, resting on green velvet, and on squarish
pedestals of varying height were statues of varying
styles—of plaster, bronze, terra cotta, alabaster, wood—
none over three feet tall. Around the walls fancy swords
were hung, and a tall, narrow, glass-doored bookcase at
one end of the room was half full of ancient-looking vol-
umes. Most of them were thick and squat, with peeling
bindings.

"It is all garbage," Menlo said, with something like
contempt in his voice. "Kapor is indiscriminate in his
artistic affections. He buys because a particular item is
for sale, not because it adds anything artistically. Look at

this gibberish! What a confusion of styles and periods. What would Kapor do with a hundred thousand dollars, if he were allowed to retain it? Create an entire house of monstrosities such as this? Such tastelessness deserves no hundred thousand dollars!"

He moved deeper into the room, frowning. "There are good pieces here," he said. "A few, but only a few. There's a Gardner over there, one of the better moderns. But in such surroundings, how can anything reveal its true value? Ah! Here is your mourner!"

It stood in a corner, near the bookcase, on a low pedestal nearly hidden from view. White, small, alone, bent by grief, the mourner stood, his face turned away. A young monk, soft-faced, his cowl back to reveal his clipped hair, his hands slender and long-fingered, the toes of his right foot peeking out from under his rough white robe. His eyes stared at the floor, large, full of sorrow. His left arm was bent, the hand up alongside his cheek, palm outward and shielding his face. His right hand, the fingers straight, almost taut, cupped his left elbow, the forearm across his midsection. The broad sleeve had slipped down his left forearm, showing a thin and delicate wrist. His whole body was twisted to the left, and bent slightly forward, as though grief had instantaneously aged him. It was as if he grieved for every mournful thing that had ever happened in the world, from one end of time to the other.

"I see," said Menlo softly, gazing at the mourner. He reached out gently and picked the statue up, turning it in his hands carefully. "Yes, I see. I understand your Mr. Harrow's craving. Yes, I do understand."

"Now the dough," said Parker. To him the statue was merely sixteen inches of alabaster, for the delivery of which he had already been paid in full.

"Of course. Most certainly." Menlo's old smile popped back into place. He walked over and handed the statuette to Parker. "As you so ably expressed it, now the dough."

He turned, looking around the room and murmuring to himself, "Apollo, Apollo—" Then he snapped his fingers. "Ah! There!" He moved through the clutter of statues, a fat man weaving lithely, and stopped at a gray figure of a nude young man seated on a tree stump.

Parker and Handy followed him, Handy carrying the suitcase. Menlo patted the statue's shoulder with pudgy fingers and smiled happily at Parker. "You see? A most ingenious solution. You have a figure of speech for this, I believe. One cannot see the forest for the trees. In this case, one cannot see the tree for the forest."

"In there? In the statue?" Parker asked.

"Most certainly! Watch." Menlo put his hands on the statue's head, and twisted. There was a grating sound, and the head came off in his hands. "Hollow," he said. "The young Apollo and his tree trunk, packed with money."

He stuck his hand down inside and brought out a
batch of greenbacks. "You see?"

"All right. Let's pack it," Parker said. Handy opened
the suitcase and as Menlo brought forth handful after
handful of bills, Parker and Handy stowed it all inside.

The bills were all loose. There were hundreds and
fifties and twenties, handful after handful, and gradually
they filled the suitcase. They made no attempt to count,
just stowed it away, quickly and silently.

When the suitcase was full, there were still some bills
left over. "Alas, I misjudged," said Menlo, smiling at the
double handful of bills he held. "Who would have
thought a small statue could have held so much?"

He stuffed the bills into his own pockets, and suddenly his right hand emerged holding a derringer, a Hi
Standard twin-tubed .22. It packed hardly any power at
all, but at this close range it could do the job as well as
anything.

Menlo's smile was now broad and cherubic. "And now,
my dear professionals," he said, "I am most afraid we
must part company. You have been of such excellent assistance to me, I truly wish I could at least repay you
with your lives. But you have already demonstrated once
your ability in tracking your quarry, and I should prefer
not to spend the rest of my life looking over my shoulder. I hope you appreciate that."

Parker and Handy both moved, each in opposite directions, but Menlo in his own way was also a professional. His face tightened as he fired twice, and both were hits. Handy slammed into the wall, and collapsed in a crumpled heap. Parker flailed backward, arms pinwheeling, scattering statues, as he crashed into a pedestal.

Menlo paused a moment, but bodies lay still, and the derringer was empty. He gathered up the suitcase and statuette and hurried from the room, a round lithe fat man in a black suit, the suitcase hanging at the end of one short arm, the small white statuette tucked under the other.

The last thing he did before he left was switch off the lights.

THREE

1

Auguste Menlo was forty-seven years of age, five feet six inches tall, weight two hundred thirty-four pounds. His title was Inspector, his occupation that of spy on his fellow citizens. During the Second World War, when he was much younger, no taller, but quite a bit thinner, he had been active in the anti-Nazi underground movement in Klastrava, spending the last fifteen months of the war living in the mountains with a guerrilla band, every member of which had a price on his head, set by the Nazis.

An underground movement is primarily a destructive social force, and only secondarily a constructive political force. Whatever political ideology is present invariably reflects the political ideology of whichever outside nation supplies its matériel. Because of Klastrava's geographical location, that outside nation was the Soviet

Union. The support originally came, for the most part, from the United States through Lend-Lease, but this was never mentioned by the Russians, who were not born yesterday.

Klastravian soil was liberated from the Nazis by the Red Army. The collaborationist puppet government of wartime having been summarily done away with, was replaced by men from the wartime resistance movement, and their political orientation was reinforced by the presence of the Red Army. Klastrava was quietly and efficiently absorbed, and shortly became one of the Soviet Union's smallest but least troublesome satellites.

Before the war, Auguste Menlo had had no particular trade, being a young man content to be supported by his doctor father. During the war, and particularly during the last fifteen months of it, he had learned a trade, though his trade at first glance seemed to have no peacetime application. Then, in early 1947, through resistance comrades, he received an appointment to the National Police. At last Auguste Menlo had found his true vocation. He did his work well, and with enthusiasm, and his promotions came rapidly.

In any religion, it is the priest who is likely to ask the most pertinent questions; and if there are flaws in the religious structure, it is the priest, being closest to it and most learned in it, who is most likely to discover them. And Auguste Menlo became, in a way, a priest of Communism. In a quite literal way, he became a confessor; in the silent and private rooms of stone beneath the ground he listened to the halting confessions of the wrong in heart. Over the years, Auguste Menlo came upon the flaws that bothered no one else, and patched them as best he could, and efficiently went on about his business.

Till someone waved a hundred thousand dollars in front of his face. One hundred thousand dollars American.

Auguste knew instantly what he was going to do, the very second he was informed of his assignment. He knew it as though he had known all his life, as though his entire career had been only a preparation for this great moment when he would come into one hundred thousand dollars American. The circumstances were too perfectly joined for there to be an alternative.

Auguste Menlo had been chosen for the job in the first place because he had such a perfect record, without a blemish of any kind. He had been married, since 1949, to a plump, practical woman, a good housekeeper and an efficient mother to his two teenage daughters. So far as the record showed—and the record was exhaustive—he had never once been unfaithful to his wife, any more than he had ever been derelict in his duty to the state. He was the logical and inevitable choice.

There is a kind of man who is perfectly honest so long as the plunder is small. This kind of man has chosen his life and finds it rewarding, so he will not risk it for anything less rewarding. And while Menlo had long since lost interest in his Anna, the occasional woman who became available seemed to him hardly much of an improvement, certainly not worth the risk of losing his comfortable home. Nor were the financial temptations that cropped up along his official path worth the comfort and security he already enjoyed. As time went by, his reputation grew and so did the trust it inspired. Who better to trust with one hundred thousand dollars, four thousand miles from home?

There is no way for officialdom to protect itself from such a man. Can a man be mistrusted for being *too* honest?

So Auguste Menlo was informed of his mission and given his round-trip jetliner ticket to the United States. Outwardly, it was the same sober and industrious Auguste Menlo who walked out of the Ministry that day, was driven home, packed his suitcase, and kissed the leathery cheek of his wife good-bye. But inside he was a totally different man. On the train to Budapest, where he would make connections with the plane for the West, he allowed himself, concealed by a newspaper, the first outward indication of his feelings. A broad and delighted smile, as infectious as a giggle, spread over his face. It made him look like a depraved and aging cherub.

The first plane took him from Budapest to Frankfurt

am Main, that foggy valley in the middle of Germany so
ill-suited to the landing and taking off of airplanes. But
they landed without incident, and an hour later he
boarded the jet that would take him in six hours non-
stop to Washington National Airport, an ocean and a
continent away. A world away.

The stewardess was slender, in Western fashion, with
pale-blue skirt taut over pert and girdled rump. Menlo
feasted upon her, his eyes bright, almost feverish, his
mouth frozen in a delighted smile. It was a foolish and
dangerous way to behave. Had the Ministry chosen to
keep him under surveillance—But the Ministry's trust
was complete, and only the stewardess noticed the funny,
happy fat man with the glazed eyes. She merely thought
he was full of vodka, and hoped he wouldn't be sick. He
wasn't.

In Washington, sanity returned to him. He boarded
the airport bus and rode to the G Street terminal, and in
the course of that ride he regained control of himself.
Until he actually had the money, he must be circum-
spect. He must be cautious.

His hotel reservation had already been made for him.
He checked in, bathed luxuriously in steaming hot
water, and rose from the tub a bright pink, round and
flushed and happy. He donned fresh clothing, and paid
his courtesy call to Spannick.

Spannick, of course, did not know the fat man's mission. No one knew what it was, save for Menlo himself and three men back home, all in the Ministry. But Spannick did know Menlo, and was cordial and deferential to the point of nausea, for who knew what the Inspector's quest might be? Spannick tried to pump him, to find out at least that it was not to liquidate himself that Inspector Menlo had traveled all this distance. But Menlo evaded his questions. The meeting was brief; Spannick offered whatever assistance Menlo desired, and Menlo declined the offer with expressions of gratitude. Once this was over he was on his own.

His orders had been specific. His primary mission was to deal with Kapor; remove him, and in such a way that there would be no troublesome questions from local police. The secondary task was to recover, if possible, all or part of the misappropriated funds. If they could not be located, too bad; the important thing was to deal with Kapor.

Those were his orders, but for Menlo the emphasis was all wrong. He didn't particularly care what happened to Kapor; let him live to a ripe old age if he wished. But as to the money—that was the primary mission.

Had he intended to follow orders, he could have done so singlehanded, with little or no difficulty. But he recognized his limitations. He knew that to get his hands on Kapor's money he was going to need experienced and professional help. Like policemen everywhere he had often diverted himself by reading American detective novels, and so had a fairly clear picture of American crime, at least as it was described in fiction. It was all organized together, like an American corporation. So Menlo began by looking for someplace to gamble.

Four taxi drivers and two doormen responded to his questions with blank looks, but the fifth cabby admitted to knowing such a place, and was willing to take Menlo there for ten dollars. Menlo paid. He was driven across the Arlington Memorial Bridge and down into Virginia, and deposited at a place that called itself Long Ridge Inn. It seemed to be an old colonial house. Menlo entered, armed with the cab driver's instructions, and found himself in what seemed a perfectly legitimate restaurant, with a softly lit bar beyond an archway to the right.

The cab driver was gone, with Menlo's ten dollars. Menlo was suddenly convinced that he had been played for a sucker. He very nearly turned around and left without saying a word to anyone, but the headwaiter was already there, armed with a stack of outsize menus. Feeling like an idiot, Menlo repeated what the cab driver had told him: "I'm looking for the action."

The headwaiter, without a flicker of expression, replied, "Up the stairway at the end of the bar, sir. And good luck to you."

So that was how he made his contact with the Outfit.

The people he talked to at Long Ridge Inn were not of the sort he needed, but he told a circumlocutious story and they assured him he would be contacted once his story had been "checked out." He left his name, and the name of the hotel where he was staying, and went on back to Washington.

Three days in the hotel room. He was living on the Ministry's miserly expense budget, and so could have distracted himself with nothing more exciting than a motion picture. But he didn't even go out for that, afraid he would miss the contact. He stayed in his room, ordering his meals from room service, and stared forlornly at the telephone. Finally, at one o'clock in the morning of the fourth day, it rang and a voice told him to leave the hotel and walk slowly west.

He was met by a Cadillac with gland trouble, huge and rounded and with drawn curtains at the side windows. It rolled along beside him for a few seconds as he walked, and then a voice from its black interior called him by name. He entered the Cadillac, feeling a moment of irrational fright, and for the next two hours was driven hither and yon about the city, while he talked with the two men in the backseat.

He intended, of course, to ask for help in getting the money, then to pull a double-cross. He didn't want any percentage of one hundred thousand dollars, he wanted it all—one hundred thousand dollars. But the two men in the Cadillac seemed so confident, so competent, and so sinister, that he was no longer sure his original plan would work. He told them the story, and they agreed to join him in the venture, offering him 10 per cent of the take for supplying the information. He smiled, in mock surprise and mock bashfulness, and told them he had been planning to offer *them* 10 per cent for performing the physical labor. They ordered the chauffeur to stop the Cadillac, and ordered Menlo to get out.

Menlo opened the car door, and then paused to remind them he had told them everything except the name of the man who now possessed the hundred thousand dollars. He told them that if he must handle the whole thing himself he would, though he had hoped for a more sensible and businesslike attitude from any American organization, whichever side of the law it happened to be on. They said they just might be able to see their way clear to letting him have a quarter of the loot, so he shut the door, sat back, and smiled. Then the bargaining got under way in earnest.

Because he found them so impressive that he was no longer sure he would be able to get away with the whole boodle, he bargained tenaciously and well, and when he emerged from the car he had the fat end of a sixty-forty split. He also had the uneasy conviction that the Outfit really intended to try for 100 per cent. Ah, well. Though the members of the Outfit were impressive in their grim stolidity, Menlo was the product of fifteen years of Communist bureaucratic intrigue, and he thought he might be able to handle himself adequately in this situation.

His assistants came to see him the following day, and slowly the operation took shape. He revealed Kapor's name, no longer having any choice, and it turned out the Outfit had an indirect connection with a maid in Kapor's home named Clara Stoper. The connection was made more direct, and when Clara was offered a 10-per cent cut she would never receive she became a willing and eager member of the group. Events progressed without a ripple until the unexpected and somewhat frightening appearance of Handy McKay, who began playing up to Clara in a manner that was definitely suspicious.

Could someone else be after the money? Could there have been a leak back at the Ministry? Could there have been a leak among the higher echelon of the Outfit? There was too much uncertainty here and that was dangerous. Menlo gave the order that Handy be taken and questioned, and from that point events barreled onward like a plane in a tailspin. Menlo had shifted this way and that, always retaining his balance by the narrowest margin, and when the dust settled, there had been a total realignment. The Outfit was no longer a part of the scheme. Spannick was dead, and Menlo's bridges were burned; he could no longer change his plans and go home now, even if he wanted to. So Menlo found himself in an uneasy alliance with the two newcomers, Parker and McKay.

Menlo had much to be thankful to Parker and McKay for. They had, initially, saved his life. They had additionally simplified the actual mechanics of the robbery, far more so than the Outfit's plan. And also they had, indirectly, reintroduced the fat man to sex.

Bett Harrow. So long, so lean, so firm! So active and eager a participant! This was what he had been looking forward to while gaping at the airline stewardess, this was what he had been thinking of whenever the hundred thousand dollars recrossed his mind. Bett Harrow.

He had waited that night till he was sure that Parker and McKay were asleep, and then he had risen from his bed on the floor. He carried his shoes and his jacket and necktie out to the hall, and there donned them, smoothing his somewhat oily hair into place with his fingers and running thumb and forefinger down his trousers crease.

He knocked softly at the door of room 512 and after a few seconds he heard a bed creak and then her soft call: "It's unlocked."

He went in. The table lamp beside the bed offered the only light, amber and intimate. She was lying supine on the bed, the covers outlining her incredibly long body, her face framed by the blonde hair on her pillow. She looked up at him with surprise. "Oh, it's you."

"You expected our friend again?" The prospect of

Parker coming down the hallway now did not please him.

"That son of a bitch!" She seemed very angry with Parker. "Get me a cigarette, will you? Over on the dresser there."

"Most certainly. I will, if I may, join you."

"Be my guest."

The tendency to goggle and giggle, as it had on the jetliner, was growing stronger and stronger. He fought it away, retaining an urbane and practiced exterior as he carried her cigarettes over to the bed and leaned over to offer her a light. Her eyes were hazel, and deep, and knowing, and they gazed up unblinking into his own. He held her gaze, and smiled pleasantly.

"Thanks," she said, and blew smoke, but not toward his face. She patted the bed next to her mounding hip. "Sit down."

"You are most kind." His weight sagged the mattress, and she slid just slightly toward him.

"What are you to Parker?" she asked suddenly.

"Ah," he said. "How coincidental. Much the same question I had in mind to ask you, though of course since you are a lady, I would have phrased it somewhat differently."

"Parker's a pain in the ass," she said. "Sorry if I shocked you."

She had. Women at home did not speak in such a manner. He smiled to cover the instant of shock. "Precision in all things, my dear. And that phrase has admirable precision. My name, which our mutual friend neglected to tell you, is Auguste Menlo."

"You told me yourself, remember?"

"Ah, yes, so I did."

"What are you so nervous about?"

"I am most sorry. I hadn't realized I was."

"Parker won't be back, if that's it," she replied.

That was, of course, part of it.

He said, "As to Parker, my own connection with him is most transitory, and for convenience only."

"I could say the same thing," she said bitterly. "I'd like to push the bastard off a cliff."

"Dear lady, how rapidly we have come to a meeting of minds."

She didn't get it at first. She frowned slightly at him as she sorted out the words, and then all at once she responded to his smile with a dazzling smile of her own. "I'm Bett Harrow," she said.

"I am charmed." And he meant it. He leaned forward to stub his cigarette in an ashtray. "Parker has told me of the statuette."

"I didn't know Parker ever told anybody anything."

"He is not a blabbermouth, no. But he did tell me of the statuette. It was, you might say, a mutual sharing of confidences. My own is irrelevant at the moment, really. We might speak of it another time, perhaps."

To have a woman like this, and in her company to spend one hundred thousand dollars. What a glorious dream! What a more glorious reality! "If I understand aright, your father has paid for this statuette in advance? Fifty thousand dollars?"

"Cash in advance," she replied. "We've got something else Parker wants too. He gets that later.

"Anything of, uh, value?"

"Not to anybody else."

"Ah. Alas. My dear, I would like to ask you a hypothetical question."

"He would," she said.

"I beg your pardon?"

"My father would pay again. If Parker didn't have the statue, and you did, and you wanted to sell, he'd pay again."

"Another fifty thousand?"

"He might not go that high. But you could probably get twenty-five."

Menlo shrugged. "I am not greedy."

"I bet you're not."

He leaned over closer to her. "Another question, my dear."

"What this time?"

"In my country," he said, "women go to bed wearing

great white sacks made of cotton. In the United States what do women wear when they go to bed?"

"Depends on the woman."

"Well, you, for instance?"

"Skin."

"Skin? You mean, no garment at all?"

"That's exactly what I mean."

"Incredible," he said.

"You don't believe me?" There was a mock challenge in her eyes, and her hands gripped the top edge of the covers.

"If you endeavor to prove that statement to me," he replied, "I wish you to be warned that I can take no responsibility for whatever might transpire thereafter."

"Is that right?" She flicked her arms, and the covers shot back, baring her to the knee.

He'd never undressed so quickly in his life. One sock was still half on when he lumbered into the bed, looming over her like a dirigible. Her hazel eyes darkened, her body seemed to grow firmer and more taut, and all at once he found himself in congress with a panther. He said a lot of things in his native tongue, until he no longer had breath to spare on talk, and from then on he merely clung.

When it was over, and they'd smoked a cigarette together and talked a bit more, he got up and began to get dressed. "I will see you in Miami. Very soon, I hope. And with the statuette."

"You'll remember the hotel?"

"It is imprinted firmly upon my memory." He took one last cigarette from her pack, and lit it. "It might be best were you to leave in the morning, as Parker requested. He is taciturn and unpredictable, and I would want nothing to go wrong."

"All right," she answered.

"Until Miami, then."

"I'll be seeing you."

He returned to Parker's room and fell into pleasantly exhausted sleep, garlanded with sweet dreams. . . .

Watching Parker and Handy at work, those last two days, he had grown more and more impressed with the way they handled themselves. He had originally planned to remain with them throughout the robbery and the getaway, letting them handle all the details, and double-crossing them only after the operation was completed. But as the time grew shorter, he revised his plans and decided to do away with them before they left Kapor's house. Through some careful and judicious questioning, he had learned enough about the getaway route and the theories behind it to be able to handle it alone when the time came. But still, he was in a strange country and involved in an operation that was unfamiliar to him, besides being aligned with a pair of the most lupine of wolves. That last day, Friday, his nervousness and excitement grew and grew until he was afraid he would explode. It was more and more difficult to hold himself in check as the day wore on toward night. They had not found the derringer stowed away beneath the false bottom of his leather toilet kit. It was more of a toy than a gun, especially in comparison with the weapons that Parker and McKay carried, but it was small enough and light enough to be safely hidden and it held two bullets. If he was careful, that should be sufficient.

Friday evening, when Parker and Handy left to steal the second car, he transferred the derringer to his coat pocket, hoping they would not think to search him again before entering Kapor's house.

McKay came back at the appointed time, and Menlo carried the empty suitcase they'd bought that day out to the car. He climbed in, saying, "Have you had a good fortune?"

"Good enough."

McKay, too, had his moments of taciturnity.

From this point, when he actually entered the automobile and sat down next to McKay, until the operation was complete, he was in such a state of high excitement that he scarcely knew his name. The operation went like clockwork, and the delight bubbled up in him, mixed deliciously with terror, in a heady combination that was almost like a drug. They drove to the house in the stolen Cadillac, they entered, they found the room containing Kapor's pitiful collection of bric-a-brac. And there for the first time Menlo saw the white mourner. In his state of heightened sensibilities he saw the mourner as being deeply meaningful and symbolic; in some convoluted way it expressed to him the end of mourning. Now at last all was within his grasp.

The head came off the Apollo, just as Clara had said it would, and inside was the money. It wasn't really money to him yet—when he thought of money, he still thought of his native currency—but he knew he would have no difficulty in getting used to these unfamiliar green bills, with their Presidents and public buildings. The money poured out of the hollow Apollo, filling the suitcase and more, like a cornucopia. In excitement and dread and anticipation and pleasure so intermingled and intense that he came very close to fainting, he stuffed into his pockets the fingers caressing the crisp green bills, and then pulled his hand from his right pocket again, the fingers now gripping instead the small deadly black derringer.

Both tried to escape him, flinging themselves about, knocking statues down, but the excitement ended at his wrist. His hand was calm and steady. He fired twice, and each went down. They *had* to go down. In one lightning bolt of time, Auguste Menlo had become invincible. His finger twitched twice; his adversaries ceased to exist. Their husks, their empty shells, lay broken at his feet.

He stowed the derringer back in his pocket, hearing the crisp crinkle of the bills again, and hurried over to pick up the spoils. The statuette under his left arm, the suitcase—heavier now, much heavier—hanging from his right hand. He was flushed, feverish, victorious. He didn't even remember turning the light off on his way out.

2

Menlo was dreaming.

First, there was a beach. There were great round beach umbrellas, and crowds of people swimming and splashing in the shallow water. Women wearing wool bathing suits and big floppy hats shading their eyes looked out over the water, and men and other women lay face down on blankets, sunbathing. There was a steady roar of sound, shouting and splashing and laughing, ebbing and flowing like the waves that trickled up the flat beach and down again. And children running, people hurrying this way and that. But it was all muted, all slowed down. The shouting and splashing sounded far off as if under water, and all the running and scurrying was like a moving picture run in slow motion.

A woman came walking toward Menlo across the beach. She was tall and golden and blonde and slender, with pleasing fullnesses where they should be, and she was totally nude. But no one else paid any attention. She came closer and closer to him, smiling with a smile that offered everything, and he recognized her but he couldn't remember her name. He stared at her, trying to remember, and wondering why no one at the beach was alarmed by her nudity. Then the sun got into his eyes, making them sting and water, and he closed them for relief. When he opened them again, the woman was closer, but now she was wearing Parker's face.

"No!" Menlo screamed, and in a sudden great gout of flame and smoke she disappeared. He looked out over the water, and a huge ship with tremendous white sails was racing toward him, bombarding the beach. The gouts of flame and smoke roared up all around him. People were screaming, and running every which way.

He dropped to his knees and began scrabbling in the sand, digging a hole to hide in, when a voice said, "Why not just clamp down hard on the capsule, my friend and save all that digging?"

He looked up, there was Spannick, sitting on a kitchen chair, and smiling at him. The kitchen chair was very slowly sinking into the sand under Spannick's weight.

"You're dead," he shouted, and Spannick's face changed to Parker's. He closed his eyes, knowing he was doomed. He opened them again, and he was in a motel room with one green wall and one white wall and one yellow wall and one wall of glass covered by draperies of the three colors all combined, and he was alone.

He sat up, and slowly the realization came to him that this was truth, that he was awake and the nightmare was over. His elbows were trembling, and his mouth hung open. He tried to close it, but his jaw immediately fell slack again. He tried again, and it fell slack again. He kept trying, sitting mounded in the middle of the bed like a squat pink fish, his elbows trembling and his mouth closing and falling open, closing and falling open. But reality was returning to him, and in a minute he got up from the bed and stood in the middle of the room. He was naked, in honor of the United States and Bett Harrow.

Nightmares did come to him from time to time, particularly when he had been working too hard, or an assignment was unusually difficult, like the purging of an old friend. He knew nightmares, and he knew what to do about them, how to pull their teeth and lay them to rest. The trick was to go over the nightmare detail by detail, remembering it as fully and completely as possible, discovering what part of his past experience had produced each distortion.

Still shaky, he lit a cigarette, and discovered that even American cigarettes taste foul immediately after one wakes up. Still, it should help calm his nerves. He made a face, and dragged deep.

The nightmare then. First, the beach. That was easy. It was one of the tourist beaches on the Caspian Sea; he had never been there, but he had seen such beaches in motion pictures. And in this instance it was meant to symbolize Miami Beach, which he had never seen, even in films. The nude woman. Bett Harrow, of course. Odd he couldn't remember her name in the dream. Perhaps that meant she was not an individual to him. She, and the airline stewardess, and all the women in the American magazines were simply an erotic goal, with interchangeable bodies and faces and names. One would do as well as another. He was somewhat surprised and pleased to find his subconscious so smug about his interlude with Bett Harrow.

Next, Parker's face. It had cropped up twice, each time attached to another's body. He had met the Harrow woman through Parker, of course, but with Parker's face on Spannick's body as well, there had to be a different answer.

It could be that Parker had no body anymore, Menlo having murdered it. Was some essence of Parker after him, seeking vengeance? Friends of Parker? It was hard to imagine the man *having* any friends. Besides, even if he did, what did they know of Menlo? Nothing. Only the Harrow woman, and she was already aware that he intended to kill Parker, and approved. So the double appearance of Parker's face was simply an oversensitive reaction of having eliminated such a formidable opponent. Next, the ship with the white sails. He had to think about that for a few minutes, pacing back and forth in front of the bed, and at last it came to him. Jenny's song, from *Dreigroschenoper*. The pirate ship. He had been in mortal danger from the pirates—first the Outfit, and later Parker and McKay—and this was simply a recording of that fact. And the same was true of Spannick's appearance, saying exactly what he had said in the cellar that night.

He understood the dream now, and its terror was washed away. He went over to the nightstand, picked up his watch, and saw that it was ten minutes to four. He had slept six hours, having fallen deeply asleep immediately after returning here from Kapor's house, feeling after the high-pitched excitement of the robbery and killings a lethargy unlike any drowsiness or exhaustion he had ever know before. So he had slept, purging his mind of all residual terrors through his nightmare, and now he was rested and calm.

It was time to be going. According to the getaway theory explained to him by McKay, now was the time to get started.

He showered, calm and relaxed, taking his time. He dressed in fresh clothing from the skin out, packed his suitcase, gathered up the other suitcase, with all the money in it, and tiptoed out of the motel room.

The Pontiac was there, waiting. He stowed both suitcases on the back seat, got behind the wheel, and took the road map from the glove compartment.

He wanted to travel south from here, but he was north of the city. Northeast. Was there any way to skirt the city to the east? He studied the unfamiliar map, following thin lines of roads with the tip of one stubby finger, and finally found a way to get over to the Capital Beltway. That would take him south into Virginia, where he could pick up a route numbered 350 which would take him to a route numbered 1, which ran all the way down the coast to Miami.

He laid the map on the seat beside him, and started the engine. He was not used to so large and soft an automobile, and he drove cautiously at first, barely touching the accelerator as he brought the car up the slope to the street. He underestimated and made far too wide a right turn, but Wisconsin Avenue at this point was four lanes wide, and at this hour in the morning there was no other car in sight anyway.

His progress at first was agonizingly slow. The automobile was unfamiliar to him, as were the street signs. The standard pictographic signs common throughout Europe were not used here. Instead of the usual white background and red frame and black pictorial silhouette, there were dull yellow diamonds, some bearing words and some deformed arrows. Stop signs were red octagons with the word STOP in white, unless they were yellow octagons with the word *STOP* in black. It was confusing, and a little frightening. He couldn't afford to have an accident now, not with one hundred thousand dollars in a suitcase on the back seat.

By the time he finally got to the Capital Beltway he was perspiring freely, despite the November chill, and there was a pain in his head from creasing his brow and squinting through the windshield.

But the Capital Beltway was a superhighway, like the German Autobahn. Menlo relaxed at once, sat back more comfortably, held the steering wheel less tightly. He also pressed more firmly on the accelerator. The car, bulky and soft as a heavyweight boxer out of condition, was nevertheless an eager sprinter. The car roared down the empty highway, as dawn slowly spread over the sky to his left. He was on his way.

3

He didn't hear the siren at first. He was trying to decide whether or not to stop in this little town for something to eat, and though the wailing filled his ears, at first he didn't connect it with himself at all.

He was just across the border between North and South Carolina, and it was one o'clock in the afternoon. He had been driving steadily for eight hours. This automobile was the most comfortable he'd ever driven, but eight hours' driving in any car has to be tiring. All the way across North Carolina he'd been telling himself to stop, but the desire to increase the distance between himself and Washington had up till now been stronger than his need for food and rest. He had stopped only once, to fill the automobile's gas tank and empty his bladder. That had been over three hours ago.

It seemed like a pleasant little town, this one, small

and somnolent. Except for the sunshine and the warmth, it could be a sleepy valley town in Klastrava. Sunshine and warmth. He had never in his life till now had enough sunshine and warmth. Klastrava was a mountainous country, in the heart of the Carpathians, and in mountainous lands the human settlements are always in the valleys. In mountainous lands the rain falls always in the valleys and mists and fogs lay there always. The summers are hazy, humid, muggy, the winters heavy with bronchial dampness.

Sunshine and warmth. And beautiful women. And one hundred thousand dollars.

He was far enough away now from Washington. It was safe to stop in this little town. Ahead on the right, a sign hung out from a building that looked like a railroad car. It read DINER. He had decided to stop here, and that was when he heard the siren.

He looked in his rearview mirror. The road was straight all the way through the little town, and almost empty. Behind him, two blocks away and coming on fast, was an automobile with a revolving red light on top.

Police.

He thought they'd caught up with him. He thought for one panic-stricken instant, that somehow they had traced him. The police authorities had learned about the robbery and the killings, and they had traced him in some inexplicable fashion. They had caught up with him.

The problem was, he didn't have the background to understand what was happening. In all of Klastrava there isn't one single solitary speed trap. There isn't enough tourism to support one.

He thought: *Run? Outrace him?*

No good. The police car would be even faster than the one Menlo was driving. Besides, his reading of crime fiction had told him what to expect ahead. Roadblocks. Parker and McKay had talked about roadblocks too, so they were not entirely fictional. In his own work, at home, he had occasionally found the need to order roadblocks set up and trains searched, even the borders closed.

Could they, in this country, close the borders between states?

The police car had caught up with him, was now beside him. An angry-looking, wrinkle-faced old man in a cowboy hat waved to him to pull over to the curb and stop.

One man? One wrinkle-faced old man? This couldn't be connected with what had happened in Washington. They would consider him, as the wording went, armed and dangerous. They would send more than one wrinkle-faced old man to apprehend him, if they were after him for what had happened in Washington.

He obeyed the old man's hand, and pulled to a stop at the curb, wondering what it could be all about. There might be some sort of border checkpoint where he was supposed to stop and hadn't, or some such thing. He would have to wait and see, find out what the old man wanted. If worst came to worst, the derringer was reloaded and in his coat pocket.

The police car nosed in at an angle in front of him, its rear jutting out into the traffic lane in the approved method, to keep him from driving suddenly off as soon as the old man got out of his car. Menlo rolled down the window on his side, and waited.

The old man came back toward him, walking with an odd bowlegged rolling gait, as though it was a horse he'd just climbed down from instead of an automobile. He was wearing black boots and dark-blue breeches several sizes too large, which sported a yellow stripe up each seam. His dark-blue uniform coat looked like the jackets worn by Army officers in the First World War. A light-blue shirt, with a dark-blue tie, and a tan cowboy hat completed him. A broad black belt, studded with shiny cartridges, encircled his pudgy waist. A heavy black holster sat on his right hip.

He came over, and stood glaring in a Menlo. "You in a hurry, bud?"

Menlo blinked. Police at home were always polite and courteous on the surface, whatever happened afterward.

He didn't know what to say. He just stared at the angry old man.

The old man said, "The posted speed limit in this village, in case you was in too much of a hurry to read the sign back there at the city line, happens to be twenty miles an hour. I just clocked you at thirty-two miles per hour, on our main street. I don't see no fire nowhere."

Menlo understood only half of it, and that half he didn't believe. "*Twenty* miles an hour?" He'd been going through cities and towns with thirty-mile-an-hour speed limits—and occasionally twenty five—all day long.

"That's what the sign said, bud," the old man said.

"I saw no sign," Menlo protested.

"It's there. Let's have your license and registration."

Impossible. He had neither.

The whole situation was ludicrous; all his high spirits and pleasant anticipations drained out of him. The United States was no different from Klastrava; no different from any other nation in the world. Mighty undertakings were blocked by petty bureaucratic insignificancies.

"Snap it up, bud. I ain't got all day."

There was no driver's license in his pocket, no automobile registration. He had only two things there: a wad of money, and the derringer. He thought quickly, trying to decide which to use.

The money. The money first. If that failed, then the derringer.

Menlo reached into his pocket, peeled one bill free, and handed it to the old man. The old man looked at it, frowned suddenly like a thundercloud. "What's this?"

It was a fifty-dollar bill.

"My license and registration," Menlo replied. He smiled tentatively.

The old man squinted, studying the bill, and then Menlo's face. He peered into the back seat, then looked the car over, front to back. "Now, what in hell have we got hold of here?" Then, with a surprisingly fast motion, his right hand snapped back, flipped open the holster flap, and dragged out an old .38-caliber Colt Police Positive Special. He took a quick step back away from the Pontiac. "Now you get on outa there, bud. You move slow and easy."

Menlo's hand started to inch toward the derringer, but the old man's trigger finger was white-knuckled with strain. The barrel of the pistol aimed at Menlo's head seemed as big as the entrance to a railroad tunnel. Meekly, cursing himself for a fool, Menlo clambered out of the Pontiac.

The old man said, "Fat one, ain't you? Turn around. Lean up against your car with your hands over your head."

Menlo did as he was told, knowing the posture the old man wanted. It was standard procedure the world around. Leaning forward off balance, the hands higher than the head, supporting the weight of the body. The position of the suspect when the police officer wants to search him for weapons. Which meant that now the derringer was to be taken from him.

How long would it be before this wretched old man took it into his head to open the two suitcases on the backseat?

And all this for driving thirty-two miles an hour on an empty street.

The old man was muttering. "I thought you was one for the judge, but now I ain't so sure. Might just be there's a poster out on you."

The old man began to pat him, searching him. The first thing he came to was the wallet in Menlo's hip pocket. He removed it, and stepped back. Menlo heard him whistle softly when he opened it; it contained money, nearly a thousand dollars in hundreds and fifties.

"Well, well, well," the old man said. "What do you know about that?" There was a pause and then a different tone. "Now, what the hell is this?"

Menlo wondered too. It hadn't, whatever it was, sounded like something the old man was pleased over. Menlo wondered where the people were. The sun was shining brightly, and this was the main street. Two cars had already gone by since he'd been stopped, both angling wide around them without stopping. But no crowd had gathered on the sidewalk. He couldn't understand it.

He didn't know that in a speed-trap town, motorists often get angry at policemen and policemen usually retaliate with a little extra humiliation such as a frisking, that in any such town, no matter how dreary, the sight of a policeman frisking a tourist is old stuff.

The old man kept mumbling to himself, and then all at once he shouted. "A Commie! A goddamn Commie!"

Then Menlo realized what the old man had found. He hadn't bothered to remove his official identification cards, and these were what the old man had been mumbling over, trying to decipher the foreign printing, until finally some sign or symbol had given the game away.

"Well, well, *well!*" cried the old man, growing excitement in his voice. "I guess maybe it's the Federal Bureau of Investigation that'd like you, bud. A big-shot Commie, no license or registration, carrying around bribe money. I guess the Federal Bureau of Investigation won't mind seeing you one bit. So you just march, bud. Get on away from that car you stole, and march. To your right. The jail's just a block away. I'll come get your car and baggage after I got you locked up good."

Menlo marched ahead of him down the street to the jail, a one-story frame structure with a blank façade, save for one small barred window and a door that had *Police Headquarters* lettered in gold on the glass.

Within, it looked like a set for a Western movie. There was a central corridor, with an office on the right containing, among other things, a rolltop desk. The door on the left was shut, and the old man had Menlo continue straight on down past it to the end, to a barred door.

It was while the old man was unlocking the door that he took his eyes off Menlo for just a second. It was then that Menlo sneaked the derringer from his pocket and fired both bullets in the old man's head.

First, he took back his wallet. Then he removed the Police Positive from the holster and tucked it inside his belt, on the left side, butt forward, where it was well concealed but he could get at it quickly. Finally, he dragged the old man's body through the barred doorway around to the other side of a desk to delay its discovery. The cells were back here, but they faced the other way. In one of them someone, probably a Negro, was singing softly and mournfully to himself about nothing in particular.

Menlo was feeling very strange. Until this moment all of his activities had been directed against the criminal elements of society, the outlaws. Kapor. The Outfit. Parker and McKay. He had been betraying his Ministry, true, but that hadn't bothered him particularly. His activity against the state had been, in a way, indirect, a sin of omission rather than commission: he was simply not returning with the money. But now he had shot down a police officer in the performance of his duty. Suddenly the break with his past was total, complete, irrevocable, much broader and deeper than he had ever imagined. Tendrils of fear began tugging at his mind and making his knees unreliable.

He had to be strong. He had made his choice, and so far he had triumphed. Whatever the obstacles, he must continue to prevail. The rules were changed now, and so was he.

He was puffing from exertion by the time he'd finished. He closed the barred door again, paused to catch his breath, and forced himself to walk casually and unconcernedly out of the building. He would not be eating lunch at the diner just ahead. He would not be eating lunch at all today.

The next major city, according to the map, was Columbia, South Carolina. He could risk driving the car that far, but there he would abandon it. He would travel the rest of the way to Miami by train. It was unlikely there would be a plane.

He got into the Pontiac, feeling the bulge of the pistol against his left side as he sat down. He started the engine, backed the car, shifted, avoided the angle-parked police car, and drove sedately out of town at twenty miles an hour.

4

It looked like a wedding cake. Menlo peered out at it from the cab's rear seat, his eyes squinting somewhat from the brightness. It was Sunday, and the sun shone bright on the Sunways Hotel, pink and white, with a great white fountain out front that looked like marzipan. The splashing water made a cool sound.

"I hate this lousy town," said the cab driver, waiting to take his turn at the canopied entrance.

Menlo, who did not answer, was glad of the delay. It gave him an opportunity to study the place, get used to it a little.

Everything was new, everything was different. Menlo's confidence had been shaken by the incident in the little South Carolina town, and in the back of his mind there was the growing suspicion that he wasn't going to make it. This was a whole new world in which he had no experience. He had no papers, no satisfactory explanation of who he was or where he came from. He had no real idea even where he was going.

There were too many things he hadn't thought of, too many things he couldn't foresee. Even in the mechanics of everyday living he was hampered by the fact that he was so brand new to the United States, and nothing here corresponded exactly with its counterpart in Klastrava. The trains he'd been on—he'd had to change twice— were unlike those at home; only one class of carriage—an open, uncompartmented, third-class type, but with upholstered seats of a first-class style. There had been no ticket booth at the entrance to the platform; tickets were taken by uniformed conductors on the train itself. From the important difference of language and currency down to the appearance and customs of restaurants, everything was subtly and jarringly strange. He had to feel his way, groping from one situation to the next, certain that everyone he met must know that he was a foreigner. In Klastrava a foreigner as obvious as he would have been under official surveillance long before this. He knew the United States was much more lax but he couldn't just blunder along this way forever, carrying a suitcase full of unexplainable money and hoping for the best.

The currency was beginning to seem more real to him now, and he was beginning to understand why he'd had so much trouble with the old man. Most Americans were

suspicious of fifty-dollar bills. He had managed with
some difficulty to spend three of them, getting smaller
bills in change, and he was using small bills and coins
now, hoping they would last until he'd figured out what
to do with the rest of the money. He realized, belatedly,
that if he'd offered the old man a ten-dollar bill instead
of fifty, there might have been no trouble.

It all depended on whether or not he was given time
to get his bearings. He needed it, and at least in the beginning he was going to need assistance. Which meant
Bett Harrow, and the statue. Bett Harrow could help
him if she chose, and the mourner should put him in the
debt of Bett Harrow's rich and influential father. That
was all he needed.

His taxi finally reached the canopy, and the rear door
was jerked open. The cab driver was paid and tipped as
was the doorman. A bellboy carried his suitcases—the
one on the left contained the money, the one on the right
the mourner wrapped in clothing—to the desk and he
too was tipped. The respectful but haughty clerk looked
him in the eye. "Your name, sir?"

Name?

In panic, Menlo heard himself saying "Parker. Auguste
Parker."

Why did they want his name, before he'd so much as
asked for a room? And why had he said Parker? On the
way over from the railroad station he had invented an

alias to use in signing the hotel register, but the abruptness of the question had thrown the name right out of his mind. So he had blurted out Parker's without thinking, adding his own first name, and in the back of his mind the suspicion that he was going to fail loomed just a little larger.

The clerk had a drawer full of five-by-seven file cards. He looked at several and frowned. "I don't seem to find your reservation, Mr. Parker."

Menlo was not that much of a traveler. His infrequent jaunts in the past had always been in an official capacity; such problems as hotel reservations had always been taken care of by the Ministry. Coming to the United States, he had been checked into a Washington hotel by the Klastravian embassy officials.

But now he was traveling on his own, and he was doing things all wrong. "I don't have a reservation. I only want a—"

"No reservation?" The clerk seemed unable to believe it for a second or two. Then a sudden frost hit him. "I'm terribly sorry, but we're quite full up. You might try one of the hotels downtown; perhaps they could help you."

Menlo and his suitcases were shunted aside. The fat man's face reddened with anger, but there was nothing he could do. He was no longer Inspector Menlo. He was now merely a hunted refugee, alone and uncertain. Even a hotel clerk could treat him disdainfully with impunity.

After a minute he went back to the desk again, and caught the attention of the clerk. "Elizabeth Harrow," he asked, "what room?"

The clerk looked. "Twelve twenty-three."

"And I may call from where?"

"House telephones to your left, sir."

The minute he reached for his suitcases a bellboy materialized, but he shook his head angrily and the bellboy went away. There was a point at which hesitancy and confusion could no longer be borne, when what was needed was a sharp, sudden show of aggressive certainty. He had pussyfooted long enough; it was not his style. He would put up with it no longer.

He even took offense at the bored tone with which the switchboard operator responded. His own voice was authoritative and brisk as he gave Bett Harrow's room number. But there was no response; she was apparently not in her room.

He slammed the receiver down with annoyance, turned, caught the bellboy's eye. The boy hurried over, and Menlo pointed imperiously at his suitcases.

"I wish to check this luggage. Are there facilities?"

"Yes, sir. Right over there by—"

"You may take the luggage, and bring me the claim check."

"Yes, sir."

He lit a cigarette. He had discovered a brand that

combined the superior American tobacco with an adaptation of the Russian cardboard mouthpiece. There was an annoying wad of cotton or some foreign substance wedged down into the cardboard tube, but it didn't alter the taste much. It would do.

When the boy returned with a square of numbered red plastic, Menlo tipped him a quarter and asked for the restaurant. The boy pointed it out, and Menlo marched resolutely through the wide doorway. He had come into the hotel looking soft and fat and slump-shouldered, but now he was his normal self again, carrying his bulk with lithe dignity.

He had steak, an American specialty. His table was next to a huge glass window overlooking the beach, and as he ate he watched the hotel guests there. A few were swimming, but most were merely walking about aimlessly or lying on pneumatic mattresses. A depressing number of the women, all in bright-colored bathing suits, were stout and middle-aged and ugly, but here and there was a tall and beautiful one, and these he watched with pleasure and a feeling of anticipation.

He ate a leisurely meal, and lingered at the table afterward to smoke a cigarette over a third cup of coffee. It was mid-afternoon, a slack time in the restaurant, so no effort was made to hurry him. When at last he paid his check, he took a chance and proffered one of the fifty-dollar bills. He was terrified of running short of the

THE MOURNER

smaller bills again, and surely here a fifty-dollar bill
wouldn't seem unusual. The waiter didn't seem to react
at all, but took the bill and soon returned with a little
tray full of change. In this country, he noted, a waiter's
tip was not automatically added on to the bill—at home
it was a standard 10 per cent—but was left to the dis-
cretion of the diner. To be on the safe side he left a 15 per
cent tip instead of 10, and strolled back out to the lobby.

Menlo crossed to the house phones and called Bett
Harrow's room again, and this time she was there. "Good
afternoon, my dear, this is Auguste."

He hoped she would recognize him by the first name
alone. He didn't want to mention his full name, in case
the switchboard operator was listening in.

There was the briefest of hesitations. "Well, I'll be
damned. You did it."

"You expected less?"

"Where are you?"

"In the lobby. I would like to talk to you."

"Come on up."

"Thank you."

There was a bank of elevators across the way. He went
over and was swooped up to the twelfth floor, where the
corridor was uneasily reminiscent of Dr. Caligari's cabi-
net, the walls and ceiling painted in bright primary colors, the carpeting wine red. He found the door marked
1223 and knocked.

She opened the door almost immediately, smiling at him in amusement. "Come in, come in. Tell me all about it."

"In due time. It is more than pleasant to see you again."

She was wearing form-fitting plaid slacks and a pale-blue halter. Her feet were bare, and the toenails were painted bright red. This struck him as ludicrous—it was as though she were wearing a flowing mustache—but he refrained from any comment. Still, it was unfortunate; the golden American goddess with scarlet toes. A bit of the glamour was destroyed for him forever. Inside her shoes, had the airline stewardess too had scarlet toes? Sad.

She closed the door behind him. The room looked like a more expensive version of the motel room in Washington. There was the same cheap bright-plastic look to everything.

"To tell you the truth," she said, as they both sat down, "I didn't expect to see you again. I thought Chuck would eat you up."

"Chuck? Ah, yes. Parker, you mean."

She shrugged. "He calls himself Chuck Willis sometimes. That's the way I think of him."

"Under any name," he replied, smiling, "he did not eat me up. As you can see."

"I hope you didn't leave him alive anywhere," she said, "I think he'd be a bad man to have for an enemy."

"We need have no fears in that respect."

She shook her head in slow amazement. "There's more to you than meets the eye, Auguste. Auguste? Don't you have a better name than that?"

"I am most sorry. Only the one name."

"It's too ridiculous to call you Auguste. And you're no Augie."

"A minor problem," he said, feeling annoyance that she should find his name ridiculous. "I suggest we table it for the moment. I have the statue."

"I just can't get it through my head. You really did kill Chuck and take the statue? What about the other one, that friend of Chuck's?"

"Both of them. It is a closed issue. The past has no lasting fascination for me. It is the immediate future which now concerns me. I should like to meet your father."

"I know, you want to sell him the statue. Twenty-five thousand?"

"Perhaps not. Possibly there is something he can do for me that would be more valuable."

"Like what?" She seemed at once more alert.

He considered his words carefully. "In a sense," he said, "I am in this nation illegally. My visa was for a short time only, and good only in Washington. It is my intention to remain in this country, therefore I will need papers. Your father is a well-to-do and influential man. It is not impossible that among his contacts is someone who can furnish me with the appropriate forged papers."

"I don't know if he can help you. If he can, is that all you want?"

"One small matter in addition. I have in my possession a rather substantial sum of cash, American. I would prefer not to carry this around with me. Your father perhaps could aid me in placing it in a bank or some other safe repository?"

"How much is a large sum?"

"I have not counted it as yet, but I believe it is approximately one hundred thousand dollars."

Her eyes widened. "My God! Did you take that away from Chuck too?"

"If you mean was it his money—no, it was not."

"All right. Anything else?"

"One more small matter. I had no reservation, and cannot obtain a room here."

"I'll see what I can do."

She went to the phone, spoke to someone at length and finally hung up. She turned to Menlo. "All set. It's on the wrong side of the hotel—no view of the ocean—but it's a room. You can pick the key up downstairs. I told them your name was John Auguste, is that all right?"

"Perfectly."

"My father isn't in Miami now, but I will call him. He

should be able to get here by tomorrow. I'll let you explain to him exactly what you want. I'll just tell him Chuck Willis is dead, and that someone else has the statue and wants to sell it."

"Very good." Menlo got to his feet. "I do thank you."

"Where are you going?" She seemed displeased. "You're all business now, is that it?"

"I have been traveling, dear lady. I should like to shower, to rest, and to don fresh clothing. I had intended to ask you to dine with me this evening, to allow me to make some small gesture of appreciation for your assistance."

"You're a strange man," she said.

"Is eight o'clock acceptable?"

"Why not?"

He bowed. "I shall see you then."

She walked him to the door and even barefoot she was a good two inches taller than him. She opened the door and stood holding the knob. "You didn't even try to kiss me."

Menlo was surprised. It was true that she had granted him her favors in the hotel in Washington, but he had thought then that it was only because Parker had rejected her. Could it be that she actually found him attractive? He was shorter than she, and unfortunately overweight, and possibly twenty years her senior.

But it couldn't be the money; she was already rich.

Surprised, not quite sure what to make of her, he said,

"You must forgive me. I have been, as I say, traveling. I am somewhat weary. And also, I must confess, my mind has been occupied with my own predicament. This evening, I trust you will find me more gallant."

"This evening," she replied, "you can tell me all about how you got the upper hand with Chuck. That I've got to hear."

"I will tell all. Until this evening, then."

He bowed his way out and took the elevator back down to the lobby. He didn't approach the same clerk, but another one, giving the name Bett Harrow had invented for him. John Auguste. It would do as well as any. The clerk handed him the key, and a bellboy went to reclaim his luggage.

He had intended to bathe first, but once the bellboy had left the room he found his curiosity could wait no longer. How much exactly *did* he have in the suitcase?

When he opened it on the bed, loose bills spilled out on all sides. Hundreds, fifties, some twenties. With a flutter in his chest, as though he were standing too close to the edge of a cliff and looking over, he sat down on the bed and began to count. His weight depressed the mattress, tilting the suitcase, and another little shower of bills fluttered to the bedspread.

He made a little game out of it. First, he separated the bills into three piles, by denomination. Then, beginning

with the hundreds, he sorted them into stacks, twenty-
five bills in each.

Seven hundred fifty-three hundreds.

Four hundred twenty-two fifties.

And one hundred seventy-four twenties.

Nine-nine thousand, eight hundred eighty dollars.
$99,880.00. Nine nine comma eight eight zero decimal
zero zero. In the currency of his native land, three mil-
lion, one hundred ninety-six thousand, one hundred
sixty koter.

Oh, and more. In his wallet was eight hundred and
fifty-three dollars. In his coat pocket, five hundred more.
He had spent, coming down, he estimated approximately a hundred dollars.

Grand total: One hundred and one thousand, three
hundred and thirty-three dollars!

He sang gaily in the shower. In English.

5

He was awakened the next afternoon on the beach by a funereal man in black who asked if he was Mr. John Auguste.

He opened his eyes, but immediately closed them again, against the glare of the sun. He had seen only the funereal man in black, in silhouette, bending over him, blotting out part of the sky.

Mr. John Auguste? Some mistake. I am Auguste Menlo. The similarity of—

No!

He sat bolt upright, not sure for a second whether he'd actually said the words aloud or merely thought them. But the funereal man in black was still standing there, bowed, patient, waiting for an answer. With the riot of colors on the beach, he looked like someone's odd idea of a joke.

Menlo said, "Yes, I am John Auguste."

"You are wanted on the house phone, sir. By the blue entrance, phone number three."

"Thank you."

The funereal man in black went away. He was wearing highly shined black oxfords, which sank into the sand at every step. He walked slowly and cautiously because of this, and looked like the Angel of Death. Menlo got up from the pneumatic mattress and followed him.

It was Monday afternoon, a little before three, and the hotel beach was jammed. All of yesterday's check-ins were already there, plus the layovers from the week before. Menlo had to cut a meandering path through them to get to the phone.

He was wearing maroon boxer-style bathing trunks. He looked ridiculous, and knew it, but he also realized he looked no more ridiculous than half the other men on the beach. His flesh had reddened from exposure to the sun, and it was just as well he'd been awakened. A little longer, and he would have had a painful burn. Tomorrow he would have to get some of that suntan lotion he smelled everywhere on the beach.

Already he was beginning to feel at home. Sunshine and warmth. A pneumatic mattress to lie on, and occasional beautiful girls in skimpy white bathing suits to ogle. Plus, of course, the one beautiful girl to go to bed with. After last night with Bett Harrow, this day of sleep and warmth and contentment was more than a luxury; it was a necessity. There was a twenty-year difference between them, and by approximately one o'clock that morning it had begun to show.

He smiled to himself, plodding through the sand toward the hotel. What a way to exercise the weight away, eh? Sweat it away by day beneath the hot sun, sweat it away by night beneath the cool sheets.

To the left of the blue entrance were the telephones, a row of five mounted on the wall, with soundproof barriers between them, sticking out like blinkers on a horse. Menlo went to number three and picked up the receiver. "Auguste here."

"This is Ralph Harrow."

"Ah! Mr. Harrow!"

"I'm told you have something to show me. If it's convenient, you could bring it up now. Top floor, suite D."

Bring it? Not quite so soon, Menlo thought. "Ah, I am sorry. It isn't, ah, completely ready to be shown; not quite yet. But perhaps I could come and discuss the situation with you? In one hour?"

There was the briefest of pauses, and then Harrow replied, "That's fine. One hour."

"I look forward to meeting you," Menlo said, but Harrow had hung up. Menlo returned the receiver to its hook and smiled at it. *Bring* the statue? Did Harrow have some idea he could get the statue by trickery, and not pay for it?

A depressing thought occurred to him. *That* might be why the daughter had been so free with her charms. To lull his suspicions, to dull his wits.

But would a father, even in the United States, use his daughter in such fashion?

He wished he knew for sure what Bett Harrow saw in him. He was not young or handsome, he was only rich. But she was rich too.

He couldn't understand it. He was grateful for it and he would not refuse it, but he couldn't understand it.

He left the telephones and went through the blue entrance—a slate walk flanked by cool green ponds full of tiny fish and screened on both sides by tall board fences painted blue—and entered the rear of the hotel. There was a bank of three elevators here, for the convenience of the swimmers and sunbathers. Menlo rode up to the seventh floor, and then walked the endless corridors to his room.

His black suit had been returned, beautifully cleaned and pressed. His freshly laundered shirts had come back, and the new socks and underwear he had bought in the hotel shop that morning along with the maroon bathing trunks were put away in the dresser drawer. He took a shower and dressed, checked the locked suitcase full of money in the closet, which had not been tampered with, and left the room. He went to the nearer bank of elevators, and when the elevator arrived, said, "Top floor."

"Yes, sir."

When he got off, he asked directions to suite D, and was told to bear to his right. He did so. The halls up here were done in pastel shades, much less violent than in the plebeian quarters below, much more restful. He walked a considerable distance before finally seeing a door of any kind, which was marked "C." After a turning he came to suite D.

A middle-aged gentleman who could have been nothing but an American businessman—or perhaps a Swiss businessman, or a Scandinavian businessman, but at any rate a capitalist businessman—opened the door to Menlo's knock. "Mr. Menlo?"

"The name is Auguste, for the moment. John Auguste. You are Ralph Harrow?"

"Yes. Come in."

The daughter, down on the twelfth floor, had a two-room suite. How many rooms this one contained was anyone's guess. Harrow led the way down the foyer into a large sitting room. Directly ahead, through French doors, was a terrace. Doors in both side walls were open, leading into other parts of the suite.

"Sit down," said Harrow. "Drink?"

"Perhaps, Scotch. And plain water."

"Right you are."

The long sofa in the middle of the room was white leather. The marble-topped coffee table in front of it was covered by a number of American magazines, tastefully laid out in a diagonal row, so that the name of each magazine showed. Menlo sat down on the sofa, feeling the whoosh of air leaving the cushion, and looked around. He would have to get a suite like this for himself soon. Once everything had been straightened out.

Harrow brought his Scotch and water, along with a drink for himself in his other hand. He sat down at the opposite end of the sofa. "My daughter tells me you took the statue away from Willis."

"In a manner of speaking." Menlo smiled. "Actually he never did have possession of it."

"Then you're an amazing man. Willis didn't strike me as the kind of man you could take things from. Well. But that's not why you're here. You realize I paid for the statue once, don't you?"

"So I understand."

"Fifty thousand. Willis must have had that on him too. You mean to say you didn't get it?"

"No, I did not. An oversight, possibly."

"Bett tells me you have money. Quite a bit of it. In cash."

"From another source entirely, I assure you."

Harrow waved that aside. "The point is, I've already

paid for the damn thing. I don't like the idea of paying twice."

"Your daughter didn't explain my terms?"

"No, she didn't."

Menlo outlined them quickly; a safe place for his money, the necessary papers to explain himself should it ever become necessary. "And one last thing," he said. "One of my teeth is capped, and within the cap is a tiny capsule containing poison. I don't believe—"

"Poison!"

"Yes. I don't be—"

"What on earth for?"

"In my former job it was thought I might find it necessary to take my own life under certain conditions. I somehow do not believe that will ever be necessary now."

"Good God, man, poison! What happens when you eat?"

"In normal activity of the jaw, the capsule cannot be broken. But what I would like, if possible, is to have some dental surgeon remove it. If you could obtain for me a dentist who would not ask a lot of questions, I would be most grateful, most grateful."

"I think that could be arranged," Harrow said, nodding. "I'll speak to my own dentist about it. He's a good man; I've known him for years."

"Excellent. And the other items?"

"No problem at all. We'll get you the papers first, and

then dispose of the funds. Some you'll want to invest, no doubt, and the balance you'll want handy for living expenses. No problem."

"Very good."

"But now," Harrow said, "I have my terms."

"Ah?"

Harrow's eyes, all at once, were shining. He leaned forward. "Before we go any farther," he said, "I want to hear the details. I want to know exactly how you managed to get the statue away from Willis, and I want to know what on earth your job was that you had to go around with a capsule full of poison in your mouth."

Menlo smiled. "I see." He had forgotten this essential fact about Ralph Harrow; the man was a romantic. It was the first thing that he had learned about Harrow, from hearing Parker and Bett talk about him back in Washington. On business matters Harrow was a total realist, but within was a strong streak of romanticism. It was the romantic, not the businessman, who had paid fifty thousand dollars for the mourner. "I will be most happy to tell all," Menlo said.

"Let me refresh that drink first."

"Thank you so much."

Menlo told it all then, from the time he had first received the assignment until he had arrived in Miami, deleting from the story only the sexual encounters with Bett Harrow and the murderous encounter with the old policeman. He talked also about his role as Inspector in Klastrava, and this led Harrow to question him about various high points in his fifteen-year career, and about his life as a guerrilla in the latter stages of World War II. Nearly an hour went by, and Harrow was still asking questions, Menlo still talking. Harrow seemed fascinated, and Menlo, like most people, enjoyed having a good audience.

But finally it was finished. Harrow thanked him for spending so much of his time in telling the story, assuring him again that everything he'd asked for would be supplied. "Now, Mr. Menlo—or should I say Inspector Menlo, eh?—now I do want to see the mourner. The statuette. Could you bring it?"

Menlo considered briefly, but he no longer had any doubts. Harrow could be trusted. He finished his drink, got to his feet. "I shall get it at once."

"Thank you. I'll be waiting."

Menlo rode the elevator back down to the seventh floor, and got the mourner out of his other suitcase. He wrapped the little statuette in one of the white bath towels from the bathroom, and brought it back upstairs under his arm. The elevator operator looked at it oddly, but didn't say anything.

He knocked again, and once again Harrow came to the door. "You were very quick. Is that it?"

"Yes, this is it," Menlo said, and bowed.

Harrow took the bundle and immediately began to unwrap it. "Go on in," he said. "Go on in." He pushed the door closed behind Menlo, and continued to stand in the foyer, unwrapping the statue.

Menlo walked past him into the sitting room and there was Parker sitting on the white sofa, a gun in his hand. Menlo took one shocked look at Parker's face and acted without hesitation: he twisted his jaw hard to the right, and bit down.

.

FOUR

1

Menlo had been too excited, back there in Kapor's house, too excited to think about checking the bodies and making sure the two of them were dead. And a derringer with .22 rim-fire cartridges isn't very much of a gun. . . .

Parker awoke to darkness, with something burning his side. He was lying on his back on a lot of rocks with an invisible flame searing his side. He moved, and the rocks made noises under him, scraping together, and then memory imploded into his mind.

They'd underestimated the fat bastard. They'd figured him to wait till they were clear of the house, maybe even clear of the city, and he'd second-guessed them. He'd dragged that crazy little gun out from somewhere, and now he was gone with the money and the mourner, and here Parker was lying on broken pieces of statues with a burning in his side.

He rolled over to the right because the pain was on the left side, and got his knees under him, then stabbed out with his hands till they hit a pedestal. Slowly he climbed up the pedestal till he was standing on his feet. He was weak and dizzy, and when he took a step it was bad footing because of all the broken pieces of statue everywhere on the carpet. He made it to a wall, and then felt his way along the wall to the end and made the turn, bumping into the bookcase. Now he knew where he was. He kept going around the wall till he got to the door and found the light switch. He flicked the light on.

Everything was a mess. The room was a mess, broken statues and tipped-over pedestals everywhere, the mourner and the suitcase both gone. His side was a mess, shirt and trousers cold and sticky with blood. And Handy, sprawled over there like a dummy dumped off a cliff, was an even worse mess. From the look of the blood on him, and his dead-white face, he was gut-shot.

Parker went over, still very shaky on his feet, and dropped to his knees beside him. Handy was still breathing, very slow and shallow. Both guns were still here, the .380 and the Terrier, lying on the floor among the broken statues. The fat bastard had been in a big hurry.

It was a good thing. If he'd taken his time, he might have done the job right.

Never underestimate the power of a smooth-talking amateur.

Parker gathered up the Terrier, got back on his feet, and lurched over to the door. He opened it, and saw light. Down at the far end of the hall there was a staircase—the front staircase, not the one they'd come up—and light was coming up from there. And, dimly, party noises.

Parker looked at his watch. Twenty to twelve. He'd been out for over three hours. Kapor was home, the party was going on.

He thought it out, came to a decision, and sat down on the floor next to the door. He kept the door slightly open, so he could hear when the party ended, be warned if anybody came upstairs.

When he pulled his shirt out of his trousers, so he could look at the wound, the pain suddenly intensified, almost blacking him out again. A kind of green darkness closed in all around him, like a camera lens closing. He leaned his back against the wall and breathed deeply until the green darkness went away. Then he looked at the wound.

The bullet had plowed a deep furrow in the flesh along his side, just above the belt. His whole side was discolored, gray and purplish and black, and sensitive to the touch, like a charley horse. The furrowed flesh was ragged, and smeared with dried blood. Fresh blood still oozed sluggishly from the wound. As far as he could tell, the bullet wasn't in him, but had scored his side and kept on going.

So he'd come out better than Handy. All he had was a pain in the side. It wouldn't even disable him badly, once a doctor had seen to it.

He looked at his watch again. Ten to twelve. The party was still going on. To his right he could hear the shallow, labored breathing of Handy. If the party lasted too long, Handy wouldn't make it.

His left arm was stiffening up. The fingers wouldn't work right. He transferred the Terrier to his left hand, so he could get out a cigarette, and the hand wouldn't hold onto the gun. It fell to the carpet. Parker cursed under his breath, and left it there. He lit a cigarette, and leaned his head back against the wall, and sat there with the cigarette in his mouth, listening to the party noises and Handy's uneven breathing. His feet were out in front of him, and his arms were hanging at his sides, the hands resting palm up on the floor. A pins-and-needles feeling kept running up and down his left side and down his left arm. His fingers on that side felt like sausages, thick and unresponsive.

The seconds limped by, dragging sacks, forming into long lines. Every line took forever to form, and then was only one more minute. Parker lit a fresh cigarette off the butt of the old one. Then that cigarette was smoked down, and he lit another fresh one. And again.

They were happy as hell downstairs.

This was six. Six times in his life he'd been shot. And this was the second time he'd been left for dead. The first time, it had been a heavier slug, and well aimed, but it had hit his belt buckle instead of his stomach, and he'd managed to crawl away from that one with only the loss of appetite for a while. In England, in forty-four, an MP had winged him when he'd taken a truckful of stolen tires through a roadblock. And three other times it had happened. He was almost as shot up as Tom Mix.

He tried to lift his left arm so he could look at his watch, but the arm felt as though it had been injected full of lead. He reached over with his right hand and grabbed his left wrist and lifted. It was a quarter after one. The sweep-second hand was in no hurry; the other two hands were just painted on.

They were too happy down there. Why the hell didn't they go home?

What if Kapor decided to show somebody all his pretty statues?

Parker grimaced, and reached over with his right hand to pick up the Terrier. He held it in his lap, and smoked, and waited. Whenever he finished a cigarette, he butted it against the wall board. There weren't any ashtrays handy.

Handy sounded like he was snoring. Blood in his

throat, probably. So maybe he wouldn't make it, and the fat bastard would be batting five hundred.

It was getting quieter downstairs. He lifted his hand again to look at his watch, and it was twenty to two. He felt as though he'd been sitting here for days. The burning had lessened in his side, and so had the pins and needles. Now there was a dull numbness, with a low throbbing pain behind it.

Quieter and quieter. He reached up and, grabbing the doorknob, pulled himself upright. The green darkness closed in again, and he waited, leaning against the wall next to the doorway, until slowly it faded away again. The cigarettes hadn't helped; they'd just made him more lightheaded.

When he could take a chance on walking, he went through the doorway and lurched across to the opposite wall, so he could lean his right side against it. He moved along, more slowly than he wanted, until he got to the head of the stairs. He peered around the edge of the wall, and he was looking down at the big front hall, with a parquet floor. The front door was open, and people were leaving. Kapor was smiling and nodding, and telling them all good-bye. They were speaking a lot of different languages, French and German and some others. Nobody was speaking English.

It took them a long while to clear out. Two or three loud-mouthed women in furs took the longest. Then the front door closed at last, and only Kapor and his butler-bodyguard were left standing in the hall.

Kapor said something, and the bodyguard bowed and went away. They were both wearing formal dress, like waiters. Kapor yawned, patting his mouth with the back of his hand. Then he took out a flat gold cigarette case and took his time lighting a cigarette. When he finally had it going, he turned around and started up the stairs.

He was short and slender and a dandy, with a hawk face and ferret eyes. His hands and face were so pale they looked as though they'd been dusted with flour. He didn't see Parker until he was all the way to the top of the stairs. When he saw Parker, and the gun, he opened his mouth wide without making any sound.

Parker said, "Keep it soft. Walk ahead of me to the trophy room."

"The what?"

"The statues," Parker said.

Sudden alarm showed on Kapor's face, and then was wiped away again. "What are you doing here?"

"We'll talk. In the trophy room."

"Shall I shout for help?"

"You won't shout twice. Move."

Kapor hesitated, thinking it over, but his eyes kept flicking past Parker toward the room where the statues were. He wanted to know if the money was still in the

Apollo. He shrugged and walked past Parker down the hall.

"Move slow."

Kapor glanced back at him. "I see you've been wounded."

"Just move slow and steady."

Parker braced himself, and then staggered over to the opposite wall. He wanted to keep his right side as a support.

Kapor walked into the room first, and stopped short in the doorway staring at the wreckage. Then he saw the Apollo, with its head off. "What has hap—"

"That's right," Parker told him. "It's gone."

Parker followed him in, and closed the door. He leaned his back against it. He would have liked to sit down on the floor again, but it would have been wrong psychologically.

Then Kapor saw Handy lying there, breath still bubbling faintly in and out of him. "Is he the one who shot you?"

"No. You ever hear of Menlo?"

"Auguste Menlo?" Kapor looked surprised, and then frightened, and then artificially surprised. "What would the Inspector have to do with this?"

"We're going to make a deal, Kapor."

"We are? I don't know yet what you're talking about."

"The hundred grand is gone. Go take a look in the statue. It's gone."

"I can see that."

"I can get you half of it back."

"Half?"

"That's better than none."

Kapor glanced at Handy. "He's dying," he said.

"If he dies, the deal's off."

"What deal? Say what you've got to say."

"I can tell you things you want to know. And I can get you half the dough back. That's what I do for you. What you do for me—you get a doctor who won't make a police report on bullet wounds. In your job, you must know a doctor like that."

Kapor nodded briefly. His eyes were wary.

"You also take care of my partner. Keep him here till he's on his feet. When he's well enough to travel, I give you your dough back."

"How do I know you can get it back?"

"I know who's got it, and where he's going."

"You seem sure."

"I am sure. He's too greedy not to go there."

"Whatever that may mean. This other point. You said you could tell me something I might want to know. What would that be?"

"Is it a deal?"

"How do I know, until I've heard what you have to tell me?"

"Forget that part. That's bonus. For half the dough back, is it a deal?"

Kapor shrugged, and looked at Handy. "I think he will die anyway. Then you won't get me the money."

"So make up your mind quick. The sooner he sees a doctor, the better."

"If he is going to die, and I get no money, why should I deal with you?"

"It's worth the chance."

"Possibly."

"Definitely. You don't have a week to think it over."

"Very true. All right, it's a deal."

"I want a doctor. Fast. For him, to keep him alive. And for me, to tape me up so I can travel. If I can't travel, I can't get you your dough back."

"Now, what do you have to tell me that I want to know?"

"After the doctor gets here. Where do I find a bed?"

"I see." Kapor smiled thinly. "There is no trust wasted between us, eh? Am I permitted to know a name by which I may call you?"

"Pick one you like."

"Of course. You may use the bedroom directly across the hall. As to your friend, I do not think we should move him without medical advice."

"That's right."

Parker slid over until he was clear of the door, then opened it and went out to the hallway. He angled over to the opposite doorway, shoved the door open, found the light switch. He didn't see anything else in the room at all, only the bed. He went over and dropped down onto it and rolled over onto his back. He kept the gun in his hand. He closed his eyes, because the ceiling light made them burn, but he wouldn't let himself lose consciousness.

After a while, he heard a movement and opened his eyes. Kapor had come in. "I've called the doctor. I'll have him look at your friend first, of course." Kapor switched on a table lamp beside the bed, then went over and turned off the ceiling light. "That will be more restful," he said. "When you see the doctor, it might be best to tell him nothing."

"Don't worry."

"I seem to have much to worry about. But I will try to take your advice."

He left, and Parker lay there, gripping the gun and holding to consciousness. The green darkness closed down around him again, leaving only one small opening in the center. He lay that way, suspended, not awake and not asleep, until the doctor came in.

The doctor was a stocky man with a brown mustache.

He looked angry. He didn't say anything at first, then he said, "Put that damn gun away."

Parker said, "No."

"No? Then take your finger off the trigger. I'm going to hurt you, and I don't want to get shot for it."

Parker's right hand was now sluggish too. He had trouble making the fingers open, but they finally did, and the gun fell. He couldn't find it again, but he knew it was on the bed somewhere.

"Don't scream now, for God's sake." Then the doctor did something painful to Parker's left side.

It woke him up. He went from the green darkness through complete awareness to a blazing red darkness on the other side. The pain subsided, and he slid softly back into the green. Then the doctor was at him again, and it was red again. He kept alternating between the two, but he didn't scream.

The doctor, or somebody, had stripped him, and rolled him over this way and that. He felt total awareness just beyond his grasp, as though any second he might be perfectly all right, his old self again. But he could never quite make it that last fraction of an inch; he just kept shuttling back and forth.

It went on and on, and there were times when he was out completely. Then, from very far away, he heard the doctor say, "You'll live. You'll be stiff in the morning, but you'll live."

He tried to answer, but it wouldn't work. He was falling down into the green again. The green got darker and darker, and then it was black, and then it wasn't anything.

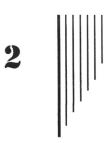

2

After breakfast, he smoked a Russian cigarette. It was about three times as long as a cigarette ought to be, but most of it was a hollow cardboard tube. By the time the smoke got from the tobacco to his mouth, it tasted exactly like cardboard tube.

The maid had said nothing to him when she'd brought the tray, and she was just as uncommunicative when she came to take it away again. It hadn't taken Kapor long to replace Clara Stoper, and it hadn't taken the replacement long to learn to be a dummy.

After she took the tray, Parker stubbed out the Russian cigarette and tried getting out of bed. Practically his whole torso was taped, giving him a tight, corseted feeling, and his left arm still felt heavier and more sluggish than usual. He felt faint twinges in his left side when he swung his legs over, a minute of dizziness when he got to his feet, and his whole body was stiff, as though he'd been given a workover by experts. He took a step away from the bed, and then stopped when he saw the two suitcases standing there at the foot of the bed. One belonged to him, the other belonged to Handy.

He was still standing there looking at them when the door opened and Kapor came in "Ah! You're up and about. Very good."

Parker was wearing only shorts and bandages. "What happened to my suit?" he asked.

"All of your clothing was burned last night, except for your socks and shoes, there at the foot of the bed. The suit and shirt were ruined."

"Where'd the luggage come from?"

"Your motel room, of course. I found the key in your pocket, and sent someone there this morning to check you out. You seem to carry identification under several different names. I assume none of the names is accurate."

"You went through my stuff?"

"Of course," Kapor shrugged. "Could you expect anything else? Perhaps you'd better sit down for a while."

Parker thought the same thing. He sank down on the edge of the bed. "What about my partner?"

"The doctor is with him now. He says he can't tell one way or the other until the bullet is removed, and it couldn't be last night because your friend was in shock.

The doctor returned this morning. He is doing what he can to ready your friend for the operation."

"All right."

"He is a good man, I assure you. If your friend's life can be saved, he will save it."

"That's good."

"And now," Kapor said, "perhaps it is time we talked."

"I want some clothes on first."

"Of course. I apologize. I confess I've been thinking more about my own loss than of yours. Which bag is yours?"

Parker pointed. "That one."

Kapor lifted it and put it on the bed. "Do you feel capable of walking?"

"Yes."

"Then, when you are ready, you'll find me downstairs. Down the front staircase, and to your left."

"All right. Wait. Where's my gun?"

"Both guns are in the top dresser drawer. I put them there to avoid alarming the help."

"O.K."

Kapor smiled thinly, bowed, and left the room.

Parker dressed slowly, hampered by his stiffness and weakness. He needed a shave, and wanted to wash his face, but that could wait. He went out to the hall and downstairs, feeling better the more he moved. He turned left at the foot of the stairs and through a tall doorway into a large sitting room with a bar at the far end. Kapor was there, mixing himself something complicated, with sugar. He looked over. "Ah, there you are. Would you care for a drink?"

"Bourbon."

"Medicinally. Of course."

Kapor brought him a glass, waved him to a leather armchair, and sat down in another facing him. "Now," he said, "if you think the time has come, I am willing to listen."

"Menlo was sent here by his Ministry. They're onto you, skimming the cream off the dough you handle. They figure you've stolen around a hundred G by now."

Kapor's smile disappeared, and his eyes narrowed. "The Ministry seems to have chosen an odd way to handle the situation."

"They sent Menlo here to rub you out, quick and quiet. Find the money if he could, but mainly get rid of you. They did it that way, because any other way it might have leaked. There's a big wad of cash due here soon, and they figured you were waiting for that before you took off."

"More perspicacity than I had expected," Kapor said, grim-faced.

"They've been holding it up on purpose, to keep you here till Menlo could get to you."

"How charming." Kapor unsheathed his gold cigarette case. "Cigarette?"

"Thanks."

Kapor lit them both. "I still don't understand what happened last night. What connection have you with Auguste Menlo?"

"He'd decided to take the dough himself."

"Auguste Menlo? Incredible. He has a reputation for honesty that passes belief."

"He was never offered a hundred G before."

"Ah, so." Kapor's thin-lipped smile flashed again. "We are all human after all, eh?"

"We were in it with him. There's a lot more to it than that, but that's the way it winds up. We were in it with him. Also, a guy named Spannick got killed when he tipped to what Menlo was up to."

"Ahh! I'd heard of his death, of course. He was at some unlikely address—But go on."

"Menlo found out where you'd stashed the dough."

"How?"

"Your maid, Clara Stoper."

"I see. She hasn't been here the last few days."

"She's dead."

"So much violence going on, all around me, and I never knew. And I was its target all along. It's a frightening thought. So you came here last night and Menlo double-crossed you."

"That's it."

"And now you say you know where to find him?"

"Right."

"How?"

"That's my business."

"Ah. Of course." Kapor settled back in his chair, smoking and gazing thoughtfully over Parker's head. "If I want any of my money at all, I suppose I had best go along with you."

"That's right."

"I imagine you plan to kill Menlo?"

"Yes."

"Please do a better job on him than he did on you."

"Don't worry."

"Not about that, no. But about this other matter. How long do I have before the Ministry decides to send someone else?"

"I don't know."

"Are they aware of Menlo's change of heart?"

"I don't think so. Spannick found out, but he's dead. Menlo claimed Spannick wouldn't have reported to them until he'd taken care of things."

"That sounds logical. Spannick was the ultimate egotist. But how did he find out in the first place? If he did, won't others?"

"No. It was an earlier double-cross, before my partner and I came in on it."

"It sounds so complex. I have the feeling I've heard barely a quarter of the story."

Parker shrugged. "You heard all of your part."

"Yes. Economy in all things. I assume Menlo has left Washington?"

"Yes."

"Do you feel strong enough to travel?"

"I think so."

"Will you want anyone with you? I can offer you one or two willing helpers."

"I can handle it myself."

"Yes, I suppose you can. Very well, then. Can I make any sort of travel reservations for you?"

"Yes. The first plane I can get to Miami."

"Miami! He's spending my money already, is he?"

"Yes."

Kapor squinted again, gazing over Parker's shoulder. "Now, I wonder," he said. "You tell me Menlo is in Miami. I wonder—"

"Forget it. Miami is a big town. I know *where* in Miami; you don't. I know who he's going to contact."

Kapor smiled sadly. "You are perfectly correct. I fear I must be satisfied with my fifty per cent. Now, one last question. How long will this take? It is now Saturday. Neither of us can be certain how long the Ministry will remain patient."

"Three or four days at the most. But what about my partner?"

"Ah, yes. If I disappear, what becomes of him? You won't return before Monday, I take it?"

"I doubt it," Parker answered.

"I will talk to the doctor. If he agrees, I will have your friend moved to a private rest home on Monday. I shall expect you to pay the bill, of course, out of your half of my money."

"It isn't your money either," Parker reminded him.

Kapor laughed. "The doctrine of private property," he said. "Don't you know that's against my religion? Nevertheless, I should prefer that you take care of the expenses of your friend's confinement."

"I'll take care of it."

"Excellent. I shall now call the airport and make your reservation. When the time comes you will be driven out to the airport in my personal car."

"Great."

"Do you want to see your friend now?"

"Is he awake?"

"No, I'm sorry to say he is still unconscious."

"Then never mind."

"Whatever you say." Kapor got to his feet. "If there's anything you need," he said, "do not hesitate to ask."

"I won't."

3

Parker moved across the crowded lobby, keeping his left elbow stuck out to protect his side, and pushed through to the desk. He signaled, and when one of the clerks came he said, "Ralph Harrow. He checked in yet?"

"Just one moment, sir." The clerk checked, and then came back. "He doesn't seem to be expected sir."

So Menlo wasn't here yet. That either meant he was driving down or he was holed up somewhere for a few days. Unless Parker had figured him wrong completely. But that didn't make any sense. Menlo had gone after Bett, to get the details of the job Parker was doing for her father. He had taken the statue. It didn't make sense any way but one; Menlo was coming down here to peddle the mourner to Harrow, probably in return for Harrow giving him some sort of a cover.

The only thing to do was wait. "Tell Freedman that

Charles Willis is here without a reservation and could use a room."

"Mr. Freedman, sir?"

"He's your boss."

"Yes, sir, I know. One moment, please."

It took more than a moment, but when the clerk came back he was affable, and Parker all of a sudden had a reservation. He let a bellboy take his suitcase and lead him up to a room on the fifth floor overlooking the beach. He tipped the boy, and then sat down in the chair by the window to rest and look out at the ocean. He was still shaky.

It was a little before noon, Sunday. He hadn't been able to get a seat on a plane out of Washington till this morning, so he'd had another night's sleep at Kapor's. The bullet was out of Handy now and the doctor thought he might even live. He'd complained about the idea of moving him, but finally agreed to it, if Handy was treated like a thin-skinned egg. So tomorrow an ambulance would take Handy to a private rest home.

It was just as well. If Kapor's bosses got tired of waiting and went in to finish him, they might decide to make a clean sweep and finish everybody in the house.

Parker had felt a lot better this morning, but the hours sitting on the plane had drained him, and now he was feeling stiff and shaky again. The wound was itching under the bandages, and there was one spot in the small of his back where the tape had got bunched up that was particularly bugging him.

After a while he got up from the chair, stripped, and looked at himself in the mirror on the closet door. His side was still discolored and bruised, but it was generally less angry looking. The tape wasn't as white and clean as it had been when it had first been put on, and it wasn't holding him as securely.

He'd had the cab stop at a drugstore on the way in from the airport, so there was now a supply of bandages and tape in his suitcase. He stripped off the old bandage, wincing as the tape tore hair from his chest, and unwound the gauze that was taped around his torso until he finally got down to the wound itself. It had pretty well scabbed over, and in this area too the coloring had gone down, though it was still pretty dark. He flexed his left arm, raising it and lowering it, and watching the flesh as it moved on his side. He could feel the strain against the edges of the wound, but in a way it helped ease the itching.

He took a shower then, favoring his left side and not letting the spray beat on it directly. The hot shower, and the stiffness, made him sleepy. He dried himself, having trouble with his left side because the skin was too tender to touch, and then he put on a fresh bandage and lay down on the bed. It was almost noon, and only a sliver of gold angled through the broad window. Parker drowsily watched the sliver narrowing, and then he fell asleep.

When he awoke, the room was darker. He forgot the wound at first and started to get out of bed at his usual speed, but a wrenching pain in his side stopped him. After that he was more cautious.

He looked out the window, and now a fat dark shadow, shaped like an elongated outline of the hotel, lay across the beach. His watch told him it was a little after three, and his stomach told him it was time to eat. He dressed and took the elevator down to the lobby.

The restaurant was across and to the left. He started that way, and then suddenly turned aside and walked over to the magazine counter. He picked up a magazine and leafed through it, glancing back, watching Menlo coming out of the restaurant.

The fat bastard looked very pleased with himself.

Not yet. It wouldn't do any good to brace him yet. Not till he knew for sure where the suitcase was.

He watched Menlo go over to one of the house phones. Menlo talked for a minute or two, and then walked to the elevators. As soon as the elevator door closed, Parker put the magazine down and went over to the desk to ask again if Ralph Harrow had showed up or was expected. The answer was still negative. So Menlo had just connected with Bett.

Parker went around to the door marked MANAGER,

J. A. FREEDMAN, and went on in. There was a new girl in the outer office, as usual, so he told her to tell Freedman Charles Willis wanted to see him. She spoke into the intercom and a minute later told him he could go in.

Freedman was barrel-shaped, five feet five inches tall. He was totally bald, with a bull neck and a bullet head. He looked hard all over, except the face, which was made of globs of Silly Putty plus horn-rimmed glasses. He came around the desk, the globs of Silly Putty settled into a smile, his hands outstretched. "Mr. Willis! So happy I could find you a room."

"It's good to be back," Parker said. His voice was softer than usual, his face more pleasant. After all these years, he fell automatically back into the Willis role.

They talked about inconsequentialities for a few minutes, long enough to satisfy the aura of friendship Freedman liked to maintain with his regular guests, and then Parker said, "There's one more favor you can do me. A small one."

"Anything I can do."

"Ralph Harrow should be checking in in a day or two. Let me know when he makes a reservation, will you?"

"Ah! You know Mr. Harrow?"

"We're old friends."

"A charming man, charming."

"Yes, he is. You'll let me know then?"

"Of course."

"I'd like to surprise him. Just tell me when he's due in, and which his suite will be."

"Certainly, Mr. Willis. I'll be more than happy to."

There was a little more talk, and then Parker left. He went up to his room and lay down on the bed to wait. He had forgotten about his hunger.

4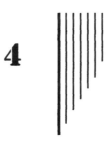

Parker heard them come in, father and daughter. Two bellboys came in with them, carrying the luggage, and Harrow and his daughter didn't say anything to one another till the bellboys left.

Freedman had given him half an hour's warning. Over the years Parker had cultivated two or three hotel employees, in case he ever needed them, and one of them had let him into the suite. He was now in the small dining room to the right of the sitting room; it was the least likely room for either Harrow or Bett to come into. If they did he could duck into the kitchen.

The connecting door was open, and he stood behind it, listening. Bett filled her father in on Menlo, explaining that Parker was dead and Menlo had the statue but was not likely to be too demanding about price. Menlo was in the country illegally, and apparently merely wanted

Harrow to help him establish a safe background for himself and also to arrange for a safe place for a large amount of cash he had with him.

"How can *I* help him establish a background? I don't know anything about that sort of thing," Harrow said.

"What difference does that make?" she said. "Promise him anything. Once you've got the statue, what do you care? What can he do to you?"

"That's too dangerous, Elizabeth."

"I don't see why. You promise to help him, he gives you the statue, and you tell him it might take a few days and then call the FBI. You give them the anonymous tip that there's an undesirable alien staying here without papers. They take him away and that's the end of it. Menlo can't ever prove you were the one who turned him in, and he can't ever make any trouble for you. He doesn't have anything on you."

"I don't know. . . ."

But Bett kept talking, persuading him, and finally he came around. She gave him the name Menlo was using— John Auguste—and his room number. Harrow put in a call and waited a minute, then hung up. "He left word at the desk that he'd be out on the beach. They'll page him."

"I'd better get out of here then."

"I'll call you after it's over."

"You want me to call the FBI, don't you?"

His voice was weak. "If you would."

"Don't worry, Daddy. Bett will take care of everything."

In a few minutes the phone in the next room rang, and Harrow spoke briefly to Menlo, who said he'd be up in an hour. Parker settled down to wait.

Menlo finally arrived, and sat down to discuss terms with Harrow. It was just as Bett had said, plus some nonsense about a dentist. Harrow agreed to everything, and it should have been over then, but all at once Harrow started asking questions about Menlo's past and Menlo had to tell him his whole life story before they were finished.

Parker, waiting in the dining room, smothered his irritation, cursing Harrow for a fool. He came close to bursting in and settling it right there, but there were two other things that had to be settled first. He had to talk to Harrow, and he had to be sure where the money was. The money and the mourner would be in the same place. When Harrow put Menlo on the send for the mourner, Parker would find out where he went from the elevator operator, and that's where he would later find the money. So he held back, controlling his impatience.

Menlo finally did leave, and the moment he was gone Parker walked into the living room.

Harrow turned, saw him, and dropped his drink. "My God!"

"Keep it low," Parker said.

"He—he said you were dead." Harrow pointed foolishly at the door. "He said you were dead."

"He thought I was. He still thinks so. Sit down, Harrow. Take a minute, get used to the idea."

"My God," Harrow said again. He went over and sat down on the white leather sofa. He pressed his left hand to his chest. "You shouldn't do that. My heart isn't all that strong."

"You want a drink?" Parker asked.

"Scotch. I think. Yes, plain Scotch."

"On the rocks?"

"Yes. It doesn't matter."

Parker made the drink, and one for himself, and came back to the sofa. He handed one glass to Harrow, and Harrow swallowed half the Scotch in one gulp. Then he breathed deeply for a few seconds, and after that he settled down. He settled down so much he looked up at Parker and said, "You're alive, but you don't have the mourner. He has it."

"You really want to go through all that garbage with the FBI? What makes you think Menlo couldn't wriggle out of it? He's a big man back home; that wasn't crap he was feeding you. He tells his boss he got the money but couldn't get Kapor because his plans got fouled up, that he was in Miami holing up until he could get back to Washington to try again. They'll swallow it, they've got no reason not to trust him. So then he's free, and there's a whole espionage apparatus he can turn around and aim at you. You call the FBI on him, and he'll make you dead. Menlo's no boy to play with."

Harrow pursed his lips, and chewed his cheeks, and stared into what was left of his drink. "You could be right."

"So instead you leave Menlo to me. He gives you the statue, then I take care of him. And he won't be coming back to bother you or anybody else."

"And what do you want for this?"

"Just the gun, same as before."

"I don't have it here."

"You better get it quick. If Bett gave you some fancy ideas about crossing me too, forget it. Menlo didn't even manage to kill my partner. He's in a private rest home in Washington, and if he doesn't hear from me at the same time every day, he'll know you made trouble for me. Then he makes trouble for you."

"From a hospital bed?"

"He won't be in it forever."

Harrow thought that one over. Finally he said, "All right. The gun is in the hotel safe. I'll have it sent up."

"After we take care of Menlo. We don't want any bell-boys coming in at the wrong time."

"No. You're right."

There was a soft rapping at the door. Harrow looked startled, and Parker said, "That's him now."

"So quickly?"

"Don't let it throw you. Just go out there and let him in. Get the statue away from him before he sees me, so he doesn't get a chance to try and break it or something."

"The statue!" Harrow hurriedly got to his feet. "The statue," he muttered, and went out through the doorway into the foyer. Parker, still seated on the sofa, heard him say, "You were very quick. Is that it?"

Then Menlo's voice, "Yes, this is it."

"Go on in," Harrow said. His voice was shaking, and Parker shook his head in disgust. "Go on in."

But Menlo didn't tip. He came on in through the foyer doorway, and stood stock still when he saw Parker sitting there. The blood drained from his face, and then all of a sudden he did something peculiar with his face, twisting his mouth around. Then he pitched over forward onto the carpet.

Harrow came in, clutching the mourner to his chest. "What did you do?"

"Nothing." Parker got to his feet. "The goddam fool. The poison."

"Poison? You mean, in his tooth?"

"Yeah." Parker knelt beside him. "He's dead all right."

"For God's sake, man, how do we explain this?"

"We don't. We stash him away in a closet or something. Tonight, around midnight, pour some booze over him and drop him off the terrace. Who's to know what floor the poor drunk fell from? Bett will be here to corroborate your story. He didn't fall from here."

"I couldn't do that!" Harrow was staring at Menlo's body with horror.

"Bett can. All right, call down for the gun now."

"But—"

"Call for the gun! Stop worrying about Menlo."

Harrow made the call, his voice trembling, while Parker dragged the body out onto the terrace into a corner where it couldn't be seen from inside the suite. He heard Harrow ask that the package that was being held for him in the safe be brought up to the suite.

They waited in silence. Harrow seemed more shaken by Menlo's death than Parker would ever have guessed. He kept working on the Scotch bottle.

After a while a bellboy came with a small package wrapped in brown paper. Harrow tipped him and sent him on his way, while Parker opened it. The gun was inside all right. Parker stowed it away inside his jacket. "Phone Bett. Tell her to come up here but don't say that I'm here."

After he'd made the call, Harrow said, "She said she'd be at least half an hour."

"That's all right. I'll be back by then."

Parker went out to the elevators. He pushed the button, and when the elevator on the left arrived, he asked the operator, "Did you take a fat man down from here about fifteen minutes ago?"

"Not me."

Parker pushed a ten into his hand. "Forget I even asked."

"Yes, sir!"

The elevator went back down, and Parker pushed the button again. The other elevator came up this time, and Parker asked the same question, with another ten in his hand.

"Yes, sir, I did. Just about fifteen minutes ago," the operator answered.

"What floor did he get off?"

"Seven. Then he came right back up here, a few minutes later."

"Wait here a minute. I want to get this ten's brother."

"I'm with you, sir."

Parker went back to suite D. Harrow wasn't in the living room. Parker found him in the bedroom, lying on his back, his left hand palm up over his eyes and his right hand holding a glass half full of Scotch.

Parker left him there for a minute, went out to the terrace, and rifled Menlo's pockets. He found the room key, and went to the bedroom. "Harrow," he said. "Get up from there. I'm going to want privacy when I talk to your daughter. You take off for a while."

Harrow sat up. He looked ashen, but he was busy gathering shreds of dignity around him. "That's not the proper tone of voice."

"Come on, I've got an elevator waiting."

"You've got an elevator waiting?" Harrow seemed bemused by the idea. He got to his feet, took the mourner up from the bed, and put it in a closet and locked the closet door, then pocketed the key and followed Parker out of the suite.

The elevator was still there, the operator patient. Parker slipped the two tens into the operator's hand and said, "This gentleman is going all the way down to the lobby. I'm getting off at seven."

"Yes, sir."

They were silent on the way down. Parker got off at the seventh floor, found room 706, and unlocked the door. The suitcase was in plain sight, in the closet, the same one they'd bought to carry the money in originally. It was locked, but a suitcase lock can be picked with a piece of spaghetti. Parker opened it, saw that it was still full of bills, and closed it again. He went out, located the emergency staircase, and went down to his room on the fifth floor. He stashed the suitcase, went back up to the seventh floor, and rang for the elevator.

It was the same one that had taken him down, and the operator smiled as he got aboard. They were old friends now; twenty dollars old. On the way up, the operator asked if he had any idea about a horse at Hialeah that could make the twenty grow. Parker told him that wasn't his sport.

He went back into suite D, this time locking the door, and returned the key to room 706 to Menlo's pocket. Then he sat down.

Bett knocked at the door ten minutes later. He went over and opened it, and she stared at him. "Come on in, Bett," he said.

She came in, not saying anything, just staring at him. She was wearing pink slacks and a white shirt and Japanese sandals.

"Come over here, Bett." He took her elbow and guided her through the sitting room and out onto the terrace. He pointed.

She looked. She whispered, "Menlo."

"How was he, Bett? In the rack, I mean?"

"You killed him," she said in a whisper.

"Better than that. Menlo killed himself. He did a better job than he did on me."

"He swore you were dead. He described how he did it. How could he get the statue away from you if you weren't dead?"

Parker went back into the sitting room, and she followed him. "You want a drink, Bett?"

"Please."

"You know where the bar is. I want bourbon."

She hesitated, and then went over and got the drinks. She brought him his bourbon and he took a sip. She couldn't take her eyes off him.

"You like the strong ones," he said. "That's the way it is, isn't it? You don't care what they look like, or what they smell like, or if they're any good in the rack or not. You just want the strong ones. Menlo was going to double-cross me, so that made him strong and you took him into your bed in Washington. Then he came down here and told you how he'd really killed Parker, and that made him the strongest of all. You have a good night, last night, Bett?"

"Screw you," she said.

He finished the bourbon and put the glass down. "I'm leaving tonight," he said, "and after that we're finished. You can't be trusted. You like to watch violence too much. But we've got hours yet before I take off."

"How did you do it, Parker? Chuck, how did you do it?" she whispered.

"Menlo's dead," he said, "and I'm alive. I've got the dough he tried to take off with. I delivered the mourner to your father. And I got the gun from him. Yeah, I got the gun. So who's the strongest now, Bett?"

He could feel it coursing through him, like electricity, strong enough to blot the twinges in his side, to make him forget any stiffness or soreness in his body. The job was over, and it was always like this after a job. A satyr, inexhaustible and insatiable. He was twelve feet tall.

He walked toward the bedroom. "This way, Bett," he said. "We've got five or six hours yet."

She followed him through the doorway, and shut the door behind her.

5

Kapor himself answered the door. It was colder than ever in Washington, after having been in Florida for a few days. Parker came in, carrying the suitcase, and set it down on the parquet floor. He unbuttoned his topcoat and Kapor said, "I take it you were successful."

"In the suitcase there. There was a hundred and twenty dollars less than a hundred grand when I got to it. There's sixty dollars less than fifty grand in that suitcase."

"I will accept your bookkeeping," Kapor replied. "May I offer you a drink?"

"Just give me the address where they've got my partner."

"Ah, yes. I believe I have one of their business cards."

Parker waited in the hallway while Kapor went into the living room. He came back a moment later carrying the card, and handed it to Parker. The place was called Twin Maples, and it was out in Bethesda. Written on the card in pencil was the name Robert Morris.

"Your friend had three driver's licenses in his wallet," Kapor explained. "I chose that one. So that's the name he was admitted under."

"O.K." Parker put the card in his pocket.

"Such a shame," Kapor said, "to be leaving this way. I am going tonight."

"Any rumbles yet?" Parker didn't give a damn one way or the other, but Kapor seemed to feel like talking.

"Not yet, but one never knows. I had hoped to leave in a leisurely fashion, and in style. My books and coins and statues would be packed, various personal possessions crated, and I would remove myself to a safe place surrounded by my possessions. But I must travel fast, and light. I have less than half the money I'd expected to be taking with me and I must leave everything I love behind. Still, I have my life and my health, and this portion of my money which you have returned to me. I shall have a head start on those who most certainly will be coming after me, so I cannot complain too much."

"I'm glad it's all worked out for you," Parker said, reaching for the doorknob.

"I'm leaving the United States, of course, at least temporarily. But perhaps we will meet again eventually, and

RICHARD STARK

perhaps someday I shall be able to repay you for what you
have done for me."

"Maybe so."

"Good-bye, whatever your name is."

"Good-bye, Kapor."

Parker went back out into the cold and walked down
the drive to the cab. He'd had the driver wait. It was another black woman in a crazy hat. Washington cabs were
full of them, driving like snowbirds looking for the Man.

Parker got in, took the card from his pocket, and read
off the address. The woman driver nodded and the cab
shot away from the curb.

On the way, Parker wondered what Handy was thinking about right now. It was a funny thing, but Handy
had been going to quit. There were a lot of them like
Handy in the racket; one more job, for a stake, and then
they'd quit. Handy had been quitting after one more job
for years.

But this time, it had seemed like he really meant it.
He'd bought himself a diner near an Air Force base at
Presque Isle, Maine, and he was planning to short-order
it himself. He'd even bought a legitimate car from a legitimate dealer and got legitimate plates for it. It was as
though he was off the kinky forever.

Parker had the feeling that this time maybe Handy
would be going to Presque Isle, Maine, for good and all.

212

The rest home was a big old brick building, with more than two maples surrounding it. It looked as though it had been somebody's estate once, but the neighborhood hadn't retained its high tone, so they'd sold out to somebody who wanted to start a rest home. Most of the patients would be alcoholics drying out or subpoena subjects hiding out. And in the middle of them, Handy McKay.

Parker paid the cab and went inside. A professional-looking nurse was sitting at a small desk in the front hallway and Parker asked her if he could visit Robert Morris. She asked him to wait, and he sat down on the wooden bench across from the desk and idly picked up a copy of *Time*. In a moment an overly bluff and hearty man came out and shook Parker's hand overly long and said he was Dr. Wellman. He asked Parker if he was a friend of Mr. Morris's and Parker said yes. The doctor asked if he knew about Mr. Morris's bad stomach condition, and Parker said only that he'd heard there'd been an operation to remove something. The doctor smiled and nodded and said yes, and the patient was coming along just fine, and that he would personally show Parker up to his friend's room.

There was a tiny elevator, an afterthought that obviously hadn't been there originally, and Parker and the doctor crowded into it and went up to the second floor. Handy's room was at the end of the hall. The doctor stayed just long enough to make sure that Handy actually did recognize Parker and had no objection to his being there, and then he withdrew, closing the door.

Handy looked pale, but he was conscious and grinning. "How are things?"

"Taken care of. Everything. I had to make a fifty per cent cut with Kapor, but the rest is safe."

"Good."

"You're going to Presque Isle, Maine?"

"You guessed it. The worst that's gonna happen to me from now on is grease burns."

Parker nodded. He dragged a chair over near the bed and sat down. "How much longer?"

"They say I can get up and start walking in a week or so. Then I'm supposed to stay here another two or three weeks after that but I don't think I will. The story the nurses have is I'm some clown who shot himself by accident, and since I wasn't supposed to have a gun, no permit or something, that's why I'm here instead of a hospital. Not breaking the law all the way, just bending it a little."

"I'm going down to Galveston for a while. When you're ready to pull out of here, give me a call. I'll send you your share. You've got to pay for this place yourself."

"I know, they told me. I'll still have enough left over for what I want."

"You know the place I stay in Galveston?"

"Sure."

"O.K." Parker got to his feet. "Give me a call, huh?"

"You bet."

Parker went to the door. He was reaching for the knob when Handy called out to him.

He turned.

"What about Kapor?"

"He's clearing out tonight. He's free and clear, I guess."

"No trouble from him?"

"No. He got half back, and that's all he cared about."

"What did he say about the mourner?"

Parker thought for a second, and then he laughed. "He didn't even know," he said. "He never even noticed it was gone."

PARKER NOVELS BY RICHARD STARK